Santa's Executive

CARRIE ANN RYAN

Copyright © 2012 Carrie Ann Ryan

All rights reserved.

ISBN: 1-62322-015-7
ISBN-13: 978-1-62322-015-0

This book is a work of fiction. The names, characters, places, and incidents are products of the author's imagination or have been used fictitiously and are not to be construed as real. Any resemblance to persons, living or dead, actual events, locals or organizations is entirely coincidental. All rights reserved. With the exception of quotes used in reviews, this book may not be reproduced or used in whole or in part by any means existing without written permission from the author.

DEDICATION

This one's for my Mom. Thanks for showing me that Christmas can happen anywhere, no matter where we live—we just need each other....

ACKNOWLEDGMENTS

I had so much fun with this book! I loved letting loose and honestly, Justin and Rina were just too cute for their own good. Thank you first to Lia Davis, my rock. You know it girlie. Kelly Muller stepped up and is one of the best Admins a gal can have. Thanks babe!

Thank you Devin, Donna, Tamara, Delphina, and Karen for reading my quirky Christmas story, even when I was afraid. Scott, as always, your talent in covers amazes me.

Thank you to my Street Pack—y'all ladies rock. Thank you for getting the word out and helping me. And lastly, thank you to my readers. I can't believe I get to do this for a living. It's all because of you. Thank you.

SANTA'S EXECUTIVE

Justin Cooper wasn't always the straight-laced Holiday Elementary School principal. In his youth, he broke all the rules and enjoyed being the bad Cooper brother. One Christmas Eve night he got a little too rowdy and things changed forever. Now the consequences of that fateful night have come back in full force and the myths of Christmas might be more real than he thought.

Anna Brewer is one of Santa's elves. Not the tiny cute little toy maker, but the sexy, petite, energy filled bombshell kind. She's come to Holiday to aid Justin in his new role as Santa's executive, but as soon as she sees the sexy ex-bad boy, she realizes the job may be more than she bargained for.

As they work together to make this Christmas one to remember, an old foe has come to town to make sure that this holiday is the coldest yet.

Warning: Contains a perky elf who dreams of something more, a Christmas myth who may be a baddie, and a sexy ex-bad boy who craves Christmas cookies…and a certain perky blonde.

Chapter 1

Sometimes being the bad boy seemed a whole lot easier. Justin Cooper let out a sigh and closed his eyes. The tension that had crept through his shoulders and neck throughout the day seemed to suffocate him. He sat at his desk in his office at the elementary school and wished he were anywhere else. Sure, he loved being the principal of his small-town school, but, sometimes, he just needed a break.

The school bell rang, a soft trilling sound that set his teeth on edge, indicating he might just get that break he wanted. It was the Tuesday before Thanksgiving, and the temperature had dropped dramatically in their small Montana town of Holiday. He'd deal with the biting cold, just as long as he got his much-needed break. A full five-day weekend all to himself.

He let out a snort. Okay, not all to himself.

He was one of five Cooper brothers, which meant he was never too alone. They'd grown up close, and he, Matt, Tyler, Brayden, and Jackson hadn't drifted apart as they'd aged like some families; perhaps because, after the death of their parents, they'd needed to rely on each other. Not to mention Matt, his youngest brother, had proposed to Jordan, bringing another family member into the fold. Being the most prominent family in town had its drawbacks. No, he was never quite alone, and everyone knew his business.

Holiday was one of those storybook old Western towns that had never quite gotten with the times and evolved. But, he was okay with that. He kind of liked having the general store across the street from his brother's hardware store. Everything was pretty much laid back and moved at a slower pace. It was a perfect pace when he really just wanted to hide away and relax. Though, in reality, he never got the chance to do just that.

He ran a hand through his too-long hair and groaned. He needed to get a freaking haircut because, according to Jordan, he was starting to look like some punk kid. And, God forbid, he didn't fit the part of a proper and professional school principal. As it was, he looked like the aging bad boy of a small town.

He was a thirty-four-year-old man who spent his life either at work or tinkering around the house. Fuck, he sounded like a whiny bastard. At least he enjoyed his job and had a roof over his head.

He worked for another hour or so on the school budget for the upcoming year and called it a day. He closed down his computer, locked up his desk, and walked out to his car, the tension never quite leaving his shoulders as he looked forward to the long weekend.

The snow had just started to fall again, leaving a light dusting on the sidewalks and cars. Everything looked like the beginning of a white wonderland, complete with Thanksgiving and harvest decorations in store windows. The one-road town appeared to be a scene sliced from an old western movie. The storefronts had been updated over the years, the road had been paved, but the town still looked old-timey. The road branched off in other directions as people built out, but Main

Street remained the center of town. The snow was light, but he knew it wouldn't take long for the sidewalks and roads to become slick. He stopped beside his car and called town maintenance, which consisted of George, his plow truck, and a few other key tools.

"Hey, I know the school's closed, but I'd still like you to salt the sidewalks, just in case. You never know what kids will want to do once they get a break." The last thing he needed was a kid to break an arm or worse. Not to mention the irate parents that would blame him. As much as he loved the kids, sometimes dealing with parents made him feel as if his job was sucking the life out of him.

George grunted, but agreed to prep the sidewalks.

Justin hung up, shivered in his coat, and got in his SUV. It dawned on him that it would have been smarter to get in the car and then make the phone call. Why he hadn't done that was beyond him. Maybe it was old age. Okay, he wasn't *that* old, but damn, he sure felt it. He slammed the door shut, shivered again, and started his car. He let it idle for a few moments while it warmed and cupped his hands over his mouth. Dear God, when did it get this cold? It hadn't been this cold that morning.

When the car was finally heated up enough that he wasn't afraid he'd kill the engine, he shifted into drive and headed home. It wasn't even that late; he just wanted to go to bed. His body felt heavy, heated, and edgy. Maybe he just needed a beer. All the more reason to head home.

Justin carefully navigated the roads, not surprised at the lack of cars. People who lived in Montana were accustomed to snow, but that didn't mean people necessarily loved to drive in it, nor did they drive anywhere, if they didn't have to. The ice was already starting to build up, and Justin knew, in a few more minutes, it would get dangerous. Luckily, he lived close enough to the school that on a warm day he could jog to work; not that he wanted to do that anymore. The leering looks from some of the single and not-so-single moms when he had done so had quickly squashed that idea.

He pulled into his driveway, parked, and then shuffled as quickly as he could into his home. Thankfully, he'd turned the heater on with a timer before he'd left, so stepping into the house wasn't like stepping into an icebox. He shook off the snow and stepped out of his shoes. He hated cleaning, so he did his best not to be a slob. He wasn't a neat freak like his brother Jackson, but he kept a clean house.

He knew his home wasn't perfect, far from it. It would always be a work in progress, at least until he had someone to share it with; another heartbeat in the house. He'd filled the rooms with heavy furniture suitable for him and his brothers. There was no feminine energy whatsoever in the home. He hadn't painted the walls yet, beyond a quick white coat, because he didn't know what he wanted. He also hadn't yet put anything up on the walls. It was as if he were waiting for something—or someone—to help him fill it. What, or who, he didn't know.

With a sigh, he strode to the kitchen and took out the ingredients for dinner. He'd been craving Christmas cookies for the past month—and given in to those cravings more often than not—so he decided on fresh salmon, rice, and yellow squash for dinner. He needed to eat healthy so he could indulge in some sugar cookies later. He didn't know what it was, but he needed sugar cookies, daily. He loved them best when they were soft and had a thick icing layer on them. Just thinking about them made his stomach growl and his teeth ache. He knew his brother, Jackson, a dentist, would absolutely kill him if he knew how many cookies he had ingested over the past month. But, he couldn't help it. He craved the suckers.

He quickly got the rice going, sliced the squash so it could steam, and heated some olive oil in a pan for the salmon. He seasoned the filet then put it on the heat, but, even as he did, visions of cookies danced in his head. Yep, he was officially going crazy. The salmon crackled and popped as the fatty tissue hit the hot oil in the skillet. The aroma of lemon and dill filled the air, and he groaned. Nope, didn't smell good enough to him. He wanted those damn cookies.

"I'm a fucking adult. I can eat a cookie before dinner if I want to." *Sure, keep telling yourself that.*

Knowing if his mother had been alive, she would have scolded him, he tiptoed to the airtight container and took out one cookie. Come on, one little frosted cookie wouldn't hurt. He hesitated, and then he grabbed a second cookie in case the first didn't take the edge off. He bit down into the sugary goodness and groaned.

Hell, yeah, this is better than sex.

He choked on the last bit of cookie and grabbed his beer to wash it down. Fuck, he needed to get laid if a cookie was better than sex. How long had it been? He tried to think about it and sighed. Damn, he was turning into the cat lady. The one that resembled the little old lady who stayed indoors all day with a shawl around her shoulders and a cat on her lap. He just needed the fucking cat.

The salmon popped again, and he rushed to the stove. Thankfully, he hadn't burned his dinner. Though, if he did, he could just eat more cookies.

No. No, that wouldn't work.

He turned off the heat and plated his dinner, and then he moved to the bar at the end of his kitchen isle and ate. With each bite, he turned the same question over in his mind: what the hell he was doing with his life? He was thirty-four years old and bored. He used to be the life of the party and celebrate the holidays like no other. Now he just did it for others. He didn't enjoy Christmas as much, either. Not since that night and that weird dream.

The doorbell rang, and he shook off his thoughts. Justin shuffled to the door and opened the it. He raised a brow when he saw who was on the other side.

"What are you two doing here?" he asked as his brothers, Tyler and Brayden, walked through the door, inviting themselves in.

Tyler took off his hat and raised his brow. He still wore his sheriff's uniform, even after a too-long day at work. His short black hair looked like it needed a cut, and his blue eyes were exhausted. "Is that any way to greet your brothers?"

Justin let out a sigh and took the six-pack of beer from Brayden. "At least you brought me something. But, really, I have enough beer as it is."

Brayden smiled, his face brightening. He ran a hand that still had car grease under its fingernails through his too-long hair and shook his head. "We always bring presents. It's the holiday season, after all. And, plus, this beer is for me and Ty; you can drink your own with that attitude."

Justin just shook his head and closed the door behind them as his brothers shook off the snow on their shoulders and walked toward the kitchen.

"Yum, cookies," Tyler said as Justin walked in behind them. He clenched his fists and held his tongue so as not to say anything. What the hell was wrong with him? It wasn't as if he minded sharing. But, for the life of him, he didn't want his brother to have a cookie, and he didn't know why.

It was as if he was five years old again.

Brayden took a seat at the bar and opened beers for the three of them. Justin took his and waited to see what his brothers wanted.

"What are you bringing for Thanksgiving?" Brayden asked as he took a swallow.

"Seriously? You ventured out in the storm for that?" Justin wiped his forehead, surprised to find it clammy. Damn, what the hell was going on with him?

His brothers shared a look.

"What?" he growled.

"Nothing," Tyler said in is smooth cop voice, the kind that he would use with a wounded crime victim.

"Sure. Tell me what's up."

"We're just worried about you," Brayden

said as he set down his beer.

"Why? I'm fine."

"No, you're not," Tyler said.

Justin let out a breath and closed his eyes. "I've just been a little tired and then weird. It's odd, but I'm fine."

"You're not turning into a ghost, are you?" Brayden asked. He didn't crack a smile when he asked.

Considering their brother, Matt, had been a ghost for the past ten years, that question had been a serious one. Add in the fact that their soon-to-be sister-in-law was a witch and the supernatural presence in their town could be a reason to worry.

He hadn't faded into the darkness, and he didn't cast spells. So, he knew it wasn't that.

"No, I'm all corporeal. But, thanks for caring," he said dryly.

"We're just worried about you," Tyler said.

Justin nodded, feeling oddly touched. But, these were his macho brothers, so he couldn't actually let them know. "Ah, thanks, buddy. Let's go watch that new tear-jerker, hold hands, and I'll get you a tampon."

"Fuck you." Tyler sneered then winked. "If

anything, Matt may need one. Have you seen how lovey-dovey, starry-eyed whipped he is?"

Justin snorted. "So eloquent. But, yeah, Jordan makes him happy. Whatever."

"Yeah, but does he have to be smiling all the damn time?" Tyler asked as he munched on a cookie.

Must not rip cookie from his hand.

"It's because he's getting laid," Brayden interjected and took a bite of a cookie.

God, are they going to eat all of them?

"More than I can say for the three of us," Justin said.

"Hey, speak for yourself," Tyler said, his palm out. "I got laid this week. More than I can say about the two of you."

"You're a pig," Bray said, a distant look on his face.

"No, I have sex with women who don't like commitments. I don't have sex every day, so back off."

"If you're so testy about it, maybe you should start thinking about settling down," Justin said. "What about Abby? Jordan's friend? She's nice, and I think Jordan wants to bring her into the family."

Tyler looked confused for a moment then frowned. "Abby? No, not so much. But thanks."

"Hey, she's nice. What the fuck is your problem?"

"She's the settling-down type, and I don't want to settle down. Plus, she's, you know, Abby."

Brayden turned toward their brother, anger on his face. "Now what is that supposed to mean?"

Tyler looked at them both and blinked. "She's just not my type."

"Oh, you mean she isn't a bimbo?" Justin asked

"Well, that's just not nice. And why are you ganging up on me? Why don't *you* settle down with Abby?"

Justin sighed. *Because Abby doesn't have a crush on me, dumbass.* But, he couldn't say that. Fuck, his brother was a careless bastard when it came to Abby, and he had no idea why.

But, that same idiot of a brother was right about one thing; Justin needed to get laid. He might not be as much of a ladies' man as Tyler, but he still needed a woman.

His brothers said their goodbyes, and Justin

was left alone in his empty home, thinking about women—and whether he should make another batch of cookies. He patted his eight-pack. He would have thought he'd have Santa's bowlful of jelly by now, but, no, he hadn't gained a pound from the dozens of cookies he'd inhaled in the past month.

Weird.

Justin sat in his armchair and watched the snowfall outside his window accumulating in large drifts. His phone beeped, and he looked down at the texts from each of his brothers saying they'd made it home. He must have been looking pretty bad if they had worried enough about him to venture out in the snow.

The holidays were coming, and he needed to get ready. Even though he didn't enjoy Christmas as much as he had in years past, he still loved giving gifts. He knew what he wanted to get each of his family members, including Jordan; not something they'd necessarily need, but something that would spark a memory or bring a smile to their faces.

Thinking about Jordan made him remember that, other than his brothers and her, he really was alone. Maybe he needed a girlfriend.

Just the thought of hooking up with anyone in Holiday made him shake his head. There were only two women, other than Jordan, in town that even sparked his interest, and those two didn't really spark it as much as make him feel as if they were family. Allison, the waitress at the town diner, was beautiful and had a great personality, but Brayden was in love with her, even if Brayden didn't know it. And Abby was like a kid sister who, yes, may be hot, but there was no interest there. God, he hated his small town sometimes.

His phone rang, startling him out of his thoughts. "Hello?"

"Hi! Justin?" a perky, unfamiliar voice asked.

"Uh, yeah. Who's this?

"Oh, I'm Rina Brewer; you're trainer. We're going to need to meet soon."

Justin blinked and looked at his phone.

Out of Range.

Uh, huh.

"Who are you again? What does this concern?"

"Oh!" She giggled. Actually fucking giggled. But, it sounded sweet and not annoying like giggling usually did. Okay, enough of the beer for him. "It concerns Santa, of course. He needs you."

Justin coughed. "Funny. I don't know you who are, but really, come up with better jokes next time. Though you do sound pretty, I'm hanging up now."

He pressed *End* as the high-pitched voice yelled at him to stop. Whatever.

He rolled his neck and stretched. His skin felt tight, achy. Something was coming. What the hell?

Chapter 2

"Oh, my God, did I actually just giggle?" Rina Brewer put down the phone and held her head in her hands. "I sounded like a freaking bimbo." She traced the edges of her pointy ears and scowled. "I hate being an elf. I have to be perky, happy, and I always have the irresistible urge to giggle like a schoolgirl. And, now I'm talking to myself. This just tops the cake of my insanity."

Oh, yes, she sure sounded like one of Santa's elves. She just needed the pointy shoes and the pointy hat to match her pointy, pointy ears. Who had ever heard of a depressed elf?

No, she had a job to do. She couldn't stand around acting like a neurotic person while there was a soon-to-be executive out there who had no idea what he was doing.

She looked down at the phone and gave a little growl. How dare he hang up on her? Who did he think he was? He was just Justin Cooper, not anyone special. *Not that you've ever seen him. After all, you've been stuck at the North Pole all your life, so quit being a second-class elf.*

Rina rubbed her forehead and sighed. She really needed to get off the pity train; it was unattractive. She picked up the phone and was just about to dial Justin's number again when it hit her: Oh, God, he didn't know. He had absolutely no idea who he was and what lay on his shoulders.

Holy peppermint balls! Someone had really dropped the ball on this one. How could they not tell him he was going to be one of Santa's executives? It was only one of the most important jobs at the North Pole, if not the world. And, no one had told him. When she'd called him up to talk about the upcoming holiday season and what job he had to do, she assumed he'd known that Holiday, Montana, was the Mecca of holiday paranormals, and he was Santa's charge.

How could he not know? Hadn't he been feeling the symptoms?

She paced around her tiny office in the basement of Santa's workshop and tried to come up with a plan. Her job was only to call up the executives and let them know the game plan. It wasn't her job to train them or let them in on the whole secret.

What if it could be? What if she could be his assistant?

Only male elves were allowed to be the trainers. That's the way it always had been, and that's the way it always would be. However, what if she could help?

She smiled and clapped her hands together, giggling. No, she had to stop that. She flexed her wrists and shook her head. She had to be professional, soothing. She couldn't be the giggling fool that seemed to be trapped in her like a wild menace.

A plan formed as she quickly donned her puffy, green coat and left her office, climbing up the stairs to the ground floor of the workshop. She opened the door to step outside, the strong wind hitting her face like an assault of the cold kind. Even though all elves had naturally rosy cheeks, she had a feeling she was even more red than usual. She walked to her little home at the end of the street, tucked in the back of the neighborhood. She smiled. She loved her little home.

As soon as she got inside, she ignored the fruitcakes stacked on the table, gifts from her too-kind neighbors, and quickly packed a bag that would last her a week. She needed to have a plan in place before meeting with Justin. She tucked wayward blonde curls back into her bun. She hated the corkscrew blonde curls; they were the bane of her existence, so she made sure they were always bound tightly against her head. Rina couldn't leave right away because she needed to make sure she at least had an inkling of what her plans were, but she also couldn't leave work right away either. Though she wasn't needed at work until after the holidays because she was only the girl who dealt with the leftover tasks, and her job lasted all year up until Santa's busiest day of the year.

Two days later, she scrawled a note, telling everyone she would be out of town for a few days, being sure to include a drawing of a giggling elf just so people would know she wasn't being abducted or anything and left it on her door in case the neighbors were worrying. Even though they probably wouldn't miss her too much. Wow, maybe she really did need to leave the North Pole.

Yes, this would work. She would train Justin and show him the New World and what Santa required of him. And then she'd show the whole

North Pole exactly what she could do. What all women could do.

It wasn't that female elves were held down and needed to rise up. Far from it. It was their species' way of life. Elves were inherently happy, perky creatures. They did the jobs that they did because they loved them. They didn't feel like they were being forced to do something.

But, Rina had always been a little different. Just like that little elf, Hermey, in that animated *Rudolph the Red-Nosed Reindeer* children's program. Unlike the animated elf in the movie, Rina didn't long to be a dentist; she wanted to be an assistant executive or a toymaker. Anything other than the female elf who filed old Christmas lists from children.

Rina made her way across town and headed toward the snow globe depository. The only way to travel, unless you had a sleigh with a reindeer, was through the magic of a snow globe. She walked in, inhaling the spicy scent of gingerbread cookies, and shook off the snow that had accumulated on her shoulders. She nodded at the older elf behind the counter and worked her way through the shelves and shelves of snow globes until she found the one she wanted, an average-sized globe with a chocolate brown base and a depiction of an old-time town, complete with the general store. She hefted her bag on her shoulder and traced the name of the town with her finger. Holiday, Montana. She couldn't wait.

With a look over her shoulder to make sure no one was watching, even though the magic in the store would know she had gone, she held the globe in both hands, shook it twice, closed her eyes, and let the snow globe take her to its destination.

Her new adventure.

She felt the magic swirl and the snow dance across her cheeks as it pulled her through space and time until she landed firmly on her feet in a small room that wasn't where she had been before. She blinked and took in a deep breath.

This was it; she'd done it.

"Oh, fruitcake, what have I done? I'm going to get in so much trouble, and Santa is going to freak out, and I'm never going to be able to live like a normal elf again." She took a couple more deep breaths. Her chest started to hurt, and she felt lightheaded. She'd never been impulsive before, no, she'd always done what she was told and put up with it to keep everyone else happy. Oh, Rudolph's nose. What had she done?

She set the snow globe down on the empty shelf in the almost-bare room and tried to catch her breath. She closed her eyes and counted to ten. When she opened them, she felt a little bit better, but she still couldn't believe she'd just left home like that. She looked down at the snow globe and frowned. Instead of it saying *Holiday*, it said *North Pole* and had Santa's workshop inside the globe.

"Huh, I never noticed that. Maybe I should leave home more often. At least once before I decided to make the biggest decision of my life. No, Rina, don't freak out; you can do this. You'll show Justin what he needs to do, and everything will be okay. Everything *has* to be okay. Now, where am I?"

With a bright smile that took a little too much effort for an elf, she left the room and walked down the stairs, hoping she wasn't in a random apartment and about to be arrested. That's all she needed, to come down to the southlands for the first time in her life and end up in jail. No, she should quit worrying. She was an elf; she was happy.

Sure.

Rina made her way to a lobby of some sort and smiled. She surveyed the scene. Based on the decorations, she surmised she was at an inn. This was great. She should have known better than to doubt the magic of the snow globe. Each snow globe went directly to a place owned by the North Pole. That way she wouldn't show up in someone's living room.

She mentally slapped herself then walked to the front desk and rang the tiny bell on the counter. A small woman with a cloud of white hair came out and smiled at her.

"Well, hello. I didn't realize we were having someone from the north today." The woman winked, and Rina let out a sigh of relief. She didn't have to hide who she was. She self-consciously adjusted the hat on her head. Even though the glamour she wore would hide her pointed ears from the public, she didn't want to make a mistake, especially not on her first day.

"Oh, yes, it was unplanned, but I still have some things to do, ma'am." Rina smiled and tried not to let her nerves show. Dammit, she was better than this.

"I take it you're here for Mr. Cooper."

Surprise went through her. "Oh, you know of Mr. Cooper, ma'am?"

The little old lady waved her hand in front of her face. "Oh, stop calling me ma'am; it makes me feel old." She winked again, and Rina smiled. "Call me Connie. I may be human, but I've seen enough go through this inn that I know my way around the paranormal. I'm just surprised it's taken this long to get to Justin."

"Call me Rina. And, yes, I'm surprised as well, but that's why I'm here." *Yes, and, hopefully, no one would find out until it was too late.*

"Well, it's good to know you. Take care of him. And, let me just say, he's a handsome man who really needs a strong woman in his life to take him in hand. So, I'm happy on that account as well that you're here for him." The woman winked again, and Rina paled.

"Uh, I'm sure he's a sweet man, but I'm not here for that." The last thing she needed was another man in her life with higher seniority.

"Oh, honey, they never are. Well, since you came here unplanned, I'm sure you don't know a lot of what goes on around here, so let me tell you. You're welcome to have one of the rooms, and I'll get it all set up for you. I also have a rental car for you. It has four-wheel drive so it will be okay in snow. You have driven before, right?"

Rina nodded, relief spreading through her that the inn was gonna take care of her. God, she was freaking idiot for coming here without knowing anything and not having a real plan.

"Okay then, we'll schedule it and you sign it, and everything will be just dandy. Now I don't think that boy knows what he is, but I'm sure you can take care of that, right?"

"Oh, yes, that's why I'm here. Everything will be okay."

Connie nodded, and Rina felt like a fool. She should just call up the main office, let them know what was going on, and try not to cry. Jack, her boss, would probably yell at her, but it would be okay. As long as Justin did what he was supposed to do, everything would be okay.

"I'm surprised, honey, that they sent you. It's just I thought most of Santa's assistant executives were male."

Not most, all. But, she wouldn't tell Connie that.

"Oh, I'm in training, but I know what I'm doing." She tried not to blush at that bold-faced lie. She might know what Justin had to do in his job, but she had no idea what she was going to do. Maybe she'd eaten some bad fruitcake the day before or something. That had to be the reason she was acting so impulsively.

Connie gave her a warm smile and explained a little bit about the town history and the tourist sites.

"Now, honey, it is Thanksgiving, so most everyone is in their home. But, thankfully, that blizzard blew past us and only left us a little bit of snow, so the roads won't be so bad for you. Now, since it is the holiday, I do believe that Justin will be at his brother Jackson's house for dinner. I'm sure he wouldn't mind for you to go down there and meet him."

"Oh, no, I couldn't meet his family like that. That would just be rude." She bit her lip and tried to think of another way out of this.

"Nonsense. The Coopers will love to have you. Plus, Justin is a little lonely." Connie gave a sly smile, and Rina rolled her eyes.

"Will you please stop trying to play matchmaker? I'm here for a serious reason. Santa needs Justin."

Connie smiled and shook her head. "Oh, yes, I know. Don't worry; I know the importance of Santa. And, I know Justin needs you. But, it's okay to have a little fun with your hard work, too, honey."

Rina blushed, but she didn't say anything. "I'd rather leave him alone on that front and we're running out of time. I think I need to start training him now." And, before anyone found out what she'd done.

"Okay, great." Connie clasped her hands together and quickly jotted down some directions to the old Cooper place, where Jackson lived alone. "There. You have fun with those five strapping young men. Though Matt is taken. He's engaged to that little witch, Jordan."

Anger sparked through her at the derogatory comment. "Excuse me, what did you say about Jordan?"

Connie's eyes widened, and she held up her hands. "No, Jordan is a witch. I meant that as a little playful thing. I love Jordan and always have.

Despite what our old mayor said about her, I knew she was a good girl."

"What?" She was more confused than ever.

"You should ask Justin about it once you get to know him better. Now get that frown off your face. I love Jordan. She's such a sweet girl and going to be the mayor of our town. She went through so much. I'm so happy that she and Matt are back together."

Rina nodded and pretended that all of that made sense to her. Connie was a sweet old lady, but Rina had to get out of there.

"Look at me carrying on. Okay, so you just take these directions, and it's really easy to follow down the road until you see the sign for the old Cooper place. It's a landmark, so you'll be able to find it. Good luck, honey. I'll be here if you need me; just like a fairy godmother."

Rina smiled and said goodbye and walked out to the rented SUV. Thankfully, all elves knew how to drive, even if they didn't need to do so up north. She adjusted the seat to fit her short stature and started on her way to see Justin. Well, not too *see* Justin but to work on him. *With* him.

Dammit. She blamed Connie for this. Yes, she hadn't been on a date in way too long, but she did not need to mess up her one chance at being something more by finding a guy to be cute.

Especially a guy who would be an executive, a job held in high regard at the North Pole.

There wasn't any snow or ice on the roads, thankfully. Even though she'd grown up on a literal ice cube didn't mean she liked to drive on the stuff. She was pretty sure the people in Montana felt the same way. Snow was piled high at the sides of the roads from where, presumably, a plow had moved it out of the way for drivers. There wasn't anyone outside walking, and only a few cars shared the road with her. It had been cold out, but it felt normal to her. Ironically, Holiday, Montana, was just about as cold as the North Pole to her. These poor residents.

She followed Connie's directions, thankfully having memorized them before she'd left. She didn't have to risk letting her eyes leave the road. She found the turnoff with an old wooden sign that said Cooper Ranch etched with a cattle brand and turned to make her way to Justin's supposed location.

Rina drove down the driveway and stepped on the brakes when she saw the house. It was so beautiful. Strong walls, a Western theme, two stories, home. Smoke billowed out of the chimney, meaning the Cooper family was enjoying a warm fire on a cold day.

Fudge sticks. She was intruding, an annoyance.

It was too late to back out now. She'd thrown caution to the wind, and now she just had to do it. She quickly parked along the side of an old Chevy, turned off the car, and got out. A cold breeze caused her to shiver, and she tightened the scarf around her neck. She looked at her reflection and smiled. Good. Her glamour was holding up, meaning no one would be able to see her pointy ears. The last thing she needed was for someone to call her freak even though everyone else, at least the elves, had pointy ears at the North Pole. She still didn't want to scare the humans. She'd seen enough TV to know that people weren't always as open-minded as they should be.

Rina took a deep breath and squared her shoulders. She could do this. She was a tough elf. Justin would get what he needed to be the best executive out there.

Confident, she walked down the pathway and knocked on the front door. The wind blew again, and she huddled into herself, hoping that they'd let her in just to get warm. Montana was really too cold for its own good. Nerves ran through her, but she ignored them. She heard laughter and groans on the other side of the door then footsteps as someone walked toward her. The door opened, and she froze.

He was beautiful.

Oh, my.

Something clicked inside. Not love, but unadulterated lust.

Strong cheekbones and a firm jaw, pale skin, and deep blue eyes made his face look like an artist's interpretation of the handsome man. He had black hair that had a slight curl to it, and those curls made her want to run her hands through it. Though his body was on the skinny side, she could see the traces of muscles through his corded sweater. He was taller than she was by at least a foot, but, since she was only five feet tall, that wasn't uncommon.

Her gaze traced his body then shot up to his face as she realized what she'd been doing. Seriously? She was checking him out, and she didn't even know who he was. Please, don't let this be Justin. She wouldn't be able to work with this man if he was Justin.

"Can I help you?" His deep voice radiated through her body, warming her.

You can help me any time you want.

Where the hell had that thought come from?

"I am... hi, I'm looking for Justin Cooper." Good, her voice sounded firm, not like the dirty elf that wanted to drop to her knees and...yeah.

The man frowned and blinked. "I'm Justin. Do I know you?"

Oh, no, no, no, no. This couldn't be happening. The first man to make her think dirty, dirty thoughts that included a lot of mistletoe and red stockings was the man she'd come here to help. This was not going to end well.

"Justin!" A deep voice from the back to house broke into her thoughts. "Who is it? What the hell are you doing with the door open and letting all the heat out. Whoever it is, let them in, and then you can talk to them. For the love of God, don't let them freeze on our porch. I don't want to have to deal with the lawsuit."

Rina blinked. Well, that was odd.

Justin cleared his throat and moved back, his arm waving to invite her in. Grateful, she walked into the foyer and sighed as the warmth hit her. Okay, maybe she'd been a bit colder than she'd thought.

"What are you?" Justin whispered.

Rina stiffened. Yes, executives could automatically tell if they were in an elf's presence, but it was still remarkably rude to point out.

"I think you know what I am, but you don't have to comment on it. You're going to need to learn to think before you speak if we're going to be able to work together."

That's good. Antagonize the man before

you completely change his life.

So far, she wasn't doing too well with this whole assistant thing. Even though she'd promoted herself. God, she was going to get fired and thrown into the wrapping department. All the bows, paper, that glitter, sequins and little toy soldiers…

She looked up and found Justin staring at her as if she'd grown a second head. Maybe she had.

"This is not going well. I'm sorry. I'm Rina Brewer. And I'm an elf."

Justin took a step back and shook his head. "How the hell did I know you weren't human before you even said anything? Since the dream? Oh, God, I knew I was feeling sick. Am I dead?"

Rina took a step forward and rested her small hands on his form. The heat radiating from him shook her, but she didn't relent. "I'm sorry. I'm not doing this very well. I have some things to say that are very important to you, okay? I know you're going to completely freak out because this is really weird. I promise you, I'm not lying."

Except for the whole she-shouldn't-be-there thing, but that was for another day.

"You said your name is Rina? How did you find me?"

"Connie down at the inn told me where you

were. I know its Thanksgiving, and you want to be with your family, but it's really important that I talk with you."

"Justin, who's at the door?" the same man as before yelled.

"It's just for me, Jackson. I meant, my friend needs help with something. Thanks for dinner."

The others grumbled, and she could hear chairs moving as presumably they were walking toward Justin. He quickly took her elbow, grabbed his coat and steered her out the door. The wind assaulted her, and the cold chiseled its way into her bones again.

"Wait, where are we going?"

"Which car is yours?" Justin asked, completely ignoring her question.

"It's the SUV over there. What's going on?"

"I'm not in the mood to try to explain to my family who you are considering I don't even know what's going on. So, we're going to go back to my place, and you're going to explain to me exactly what the hell is happening. Understand?"

She nodded and quickly got into her car. Rina gripped the steering wheel as nerves assailed her while they waited for Justin's car to heat up. Jeez, talk about adding to the tension. She followed Justin to his house, nerves rattling her. Well, at least he hadn't thrown her out of the house. It could've been worse.

They pulled into the driveway of a nice home that looked as if it were still being worked on. It was a family's home, just waiting for the family. An odd pang shot through her, but she ignored it.

She got out of the car and followed Justin as he walked through the front door, leaving it open for her. She closed it behind her and looked around the house. It looked like a bachelor's house. It had clunky furniture and nothing on the walls. It needed a feminine touch, badly. At least that meant that Justin most likely didn't have a girlfriend. That was another thing she shouldn't be thinking about.

"Okay, tell me what the fuck's going on."

"Language."

"Oh, no. You come here to my town and tell me you're an elf and that Santa needs me. I know you're the woman who called and giggled on the phone two days ago."

Rina nodded. "Remember when you were younger and you slid on the ice?"

Justin stiffened then gave a slight nod.

"Well, when you slid... you slid directly under Santa's ladder. Apparently, you hit your head really, really hard, and you almost died."

Justin gave a harsh laugh and shook his head. "No, I remember sliding and blacking out. But, I didn't almost die. Considering the fact that I was completely fine the next day, I think you got your facts mixed up, hon."

Rina narrowed her eyes at his condescending tone but continued. "No, Justin that's exactly what happened. You almost died and then slid under Santa's ladder."

"So, that meant I had bad luck or something because, hon, that's not what happened."

"Will you stop interrupting me?"

"I thought elves were supposed to be all cute and perky." He grinned a smile that normally would've sent her down in a spiral of need, but at this moment, she just wanted to slap him.

"You don't know the first thing about elves, *hon*." She stressed the last word, and he winked at her. Damn arrogant male. "But, you didn't die that night because Santa saved you."

"Right, because Santa's an all-healing god."

"No, it's because he has magic. Just like any other paranormal out there. But, there's a price for him saving you."

"What? He gets my firstborn?"

"What did I say about interrupting?"

"You're cute when you're feisty."

"I swear to God when men say something so degrading, I just want to slap the hell out of them. You're very, very lucky that I'm here to help you and not to kill you."

"So, you're an elf assassin now, are you?"

"Oh, peppermint balls!" Any attraction she'd felt for him was slowly sliding away to be replaced by the desire to hit him. Justin cracked up at her version of a curse, and she seriously thought about going outside, finding a snowball, and walloping him. "Because Santa saved you, you will now work for him. You are one of Santa's executives."

"Huh?"

"I'll explain everything, but you need to know you're in charge of a certain region, to help keep the Christmas cheer and the Christmas spirit alive. Being Santa is a very big job. It takes more than one person to keep the business going. That's why he has executives."

"I don't know who you are, but you're wrong. I'm not Santa's executive."

"Look inside and you'll know you believe it. I'm an elf; I don't lie."

Much.

Chapter 3

The water trailed down his chest as Justin stuck his head under the spray. God, he felt like someone had hit him over the head with a two-by-four. Rina had told him that his body was accepting the magic of his new role and that's why he felt so sluggish, but he felt like it had to be more than that. Magic wasn't supposed to hurt this much.

At least it hadn't looked that way when he'd

seen Jordan in action.

It had only been two days since Rina had come into his life and turned it upside down, but everything seemed so different. He rinsed out the shampoo in his hair and tried not to see Rina's big blue eyes and blond hair that she wore so tight away from her face. She'd caught a few curls escaping from their prison, and his hands had itched to wrap them around his finger. He didn't know why she kept all that gorgeous hair, or what he thought was gorgeous hair, in a bun. Maybe it was to make her look more professional? He smiled and ran the soap down his body. Considering she was maybe five feet tall and looked damned sexy with her generous curves, he didn't think the hair was working. As soon as he'd seen her on the porch, he'd known something was different about her, and then when his mind cleared, he'd needed to get his hands on her.

He let out a groan and cursed. He wasn't that guy anymore, that guy who just slept with any random woman and did what he wanted, regardless of the consequences. No, he was the elementary school principal now. He had duties. But just looking at her made him want to throw all that duty crap out of the window and see if her lips were as soft as they looked.

Her lips were plump and had a perfect little bow shape that made him want to trace it with his tongue. He groaned again and gripped his cock.

Fuck. He shouldn't be thinking about her and getting himself off. He didn't know how he was going to face her later knowing she was the reason he had to grip his cock and squeeze. His hand was still soapy, and he slowly slid it up and down his shaft, squeezing at the base. He leaned against the wall, a stream of hot water flowing down his chest as he worked his cock, harder and faster as he kept thinking about those big blue eyes and those curves just made for his hands. He increased the pace and thought of her on her knees, sucking him off. And, with that, he came, his body stiffening as he screamed her name.

Holy shit.

She may be freaking cute and sexy, but he couldn't want her. She came with all that crazy myth crap that he didn't want to think about. He turned off the rapidly cooling shower and got out to dry off. By the time he was dressed and had a quick breakfast, the doorbell rang.

Great, she was even prompt.

He tried to get the image of her on her knees helping him out while he was in the shower out of his head as he opened the door. She stood on his porch wrapped up in a fluffy coat, a matching hat, and thick scarf. She batted the lashes of her blue eyes, and if he hadn't known she was there for business, he would've thought it was flirting. It was most likely because it was cold as hell out there.

Here he was just letting her sit on the porch freezing to death. Good one, Justin.

"Come in, get out of the cold." His voice sounded gruff, and he cleared his throat.

She smiled up at him, and he bit his tongue. He had no idea what he was, what he was doing, or how the hell he was going to get through this holiday season. All he could think about was the fact that her smile brightened up her face and made him want to kiss her. It was the most frustrating thing ever. She bounced on her feet, slowly unwrapped the thick scarf from around her neck, and removed her hat. Silently, afraid he would say something stupid, like he wanted to bend her over a table or something. He took the scarf and hat from her, and he hung them up on the rack by the door. She took off her coat, and he hung it on the rack too.

This wasn't going to end well.

She wore a green knit dress. The long sleeves slid halfway down her palms and had a turtleneck so that he couldn't see any cleavage. Disappointed, he trailed his gaze down her body, loving and hating the way the dress hugged her curves. It ended about mid-thigh, and she wore thick white tights tucked into dark brown knee-high boots. She looked like a sexy wet dream of an elf. All she needed was her hair down so he could run his hands through it and wrap it around his fists.

"Justin?"

He blinked and looked into her gaze. She was blushing but looked utterly confused at his interest. He didn't know what to make of that. Did she really not know he was acting like a schoolboy and that he wanted her? Or, was she playing him, acting sweet and thinking she could get what she wanted from him? He'd spent way too many years dealing with the way too many women who did whatever they could to get in his bed. When he was younger, he'd enjoyed it. Now, after having to deal with the single, and not-so-single, moms of the children he cared for, he really didn't trust his instincts anymore. Too bad. Rina was sexy as hell.

"Justin?" she repeated.

"Oh, sorry, I guess I'm still feeling a little out of sorts."

Not a complete lie, but not the reason he was acting like an idiot. He cleared his throat and gestured for her to follow him into the living room. He watched as she looked over his belongings, an odd sense of wanting her to like them filling him. Okay, that was enough of that.

After they sat on the couch, a respectable distance between them so he didn't have the urge to see if her dress was as soft as it looked, Justin broke the uncomfortable silence. "So, Rina, what are you doing here?"

"I'm here to help you figure out what it means to be Santa's executive."

"You said that before, but I still don't know what you mean."

She gave a nervous laugh and tucked a curl back into her bun. He wondered if it would be too inappropriate for him to tell her to take her hair down. Probably.

"I know, I'm sorry. We should have started off on a better foot, but then I had to come in and steal you from your family." She gave another nervous laugh that turned into a giggle as her eyes widened. "I swear I'm not a dumb blonde, but I'm an elf. Giggling comes with the territory. I hate it."

Normally, he did, too, but coming from her, he kind of liked it. Dear God, he was a goner. "It's fine, continue please."

"Okay, before I tell you what you have to do, I want to make sure you really believe."

He gave a dry laugh and shook his head. "Do I really have a choice?"

She bit her lip then sighed. "No, not really. Why don't you tell me what you remember from that night? It's always good to start from the beginning when things are starting to change."

He really didn't want to, but he looked into her eyes and saw a determination there he hadn't seen before. It looked like he wouldn't have a choice.

"I don't remember much. I wasn't the best kid around. You could ask my brothers." That was by far an understatement. He had been an ass, a troublemaker, one of the worst of the lot, but he didn't want her to know that. He wanted her to like him for some odd reason. "I was sixteen, and I had snuck out on Christmas Eve to go get drunk with my buddies." He looked at her face and didn't see any disapproval there. Maybe she was just better at hiding it than most. "I got completely wasted, walked home, not because walking and not driving was the smart thing to do but because I didn't want to deal with the sound of the car waking up my parents. I remember trying to sneak around the back of the house to where my window was, and I must have slid on a patch of ice. From there I just remember bits and pieces of darkness and then a flash, and then I got up, snuck back to my room, and lay down."

"See? Do you remember anything about what happened when you passed out?"

"No, I thought I'd just hit my head too hard or had too much to drink. The next morning I went downstairs for Christmas and my stocking wasn't on fireplace." He gave a small smile and shook his head. "For all that I had thought I'd been sneaky, my parents had been better. They'd known I snuck out and had taken away my Christmas morning.

They said if I didn't want to act like a Cooper and a part of the family, I didn't get to be part of the family."

Just thinking about his parents, and the fact that they had died such a short time after that, made his throat close up. Rina reached out and grabbed his hand, and he squeezed back. He kind of liked having her there, having someone to talk to. Damn, he'd been lonely.

"Know what's funny? Before that night, I would have yelled, screamed, cursed, acted like a complete spoiled brat, and would have promised to change. But for some reason, the fact that I didn't see my name with the rest of my families made me feel like nothing, insignificant, and I knew it was my fault. I didn't change drastically overnight. I still had an attitude problem, but I actually *listened* to my parents after that. I still don't know why that was."

Rina squeezed his hand and nodded. "I'm not completely sure, but it might've had to do with Santa."

He snorted. Sure, the big jolly guy made him change and stop being a punk kid. Right.

"I know you don't believe me, but you should. When you were passed out, Santa saved your life. You hit your head harder than you thought, Justin." She sucked in a breath and looked as if she was about to cry.

Without thinking, he tugged her closer and wrapped his arm around her shoulders. He had to comfort her, but he didn't know why. "Hey, I'm fine now."

He looked down at her, but she didn't cry. Only gave a wry smile. "I know. I just don't like the thought of you getting hurt for some reason. Weird, I know. But, Santa did save your life that night, and as he did, he infused magic within you. That's why you were okay, and that's why you probably changed your ways and thinking, at least a little bit. You had the joy of Christmas and everything happy and jolly running in your veins, even if you didn't know it. That was bound to leave an effect, though, I'm sure your parents had something to do it. I wish I would've been able to meet them." She looked up at him, and he held back the urge to kiss her. He didn't even know her, and yet he wanted to kiss her? Maybe he wasn't as much of a good guy as he had thought.

"I think they would've liked you," he said, realizing that was true. His parents would've liked her. She said what she thought and yet had a great attitude. He was in trouble.

He cleared his throat then stood up so quickly that Rina almost fell back. She righted herself and stood near him. "Let's go get some lunch. I know it's not even noon yet, but I'm hungry." Hungry for a certain elf, but he didn't want to think about that.

"I'm hungry, too. I only had time for a quick cup of hot cocoa this morning. I did some research to make sure I had everything ready for you." Her eyes widened, and she closed her mouth as if she had said too much.

"Hot cocoa?"

"Yes, it's my favorite drink."

He held back a laugh. God, she was an elf in every sense of the word with her green dress, her giggling, and the fact that she loved cocoa. It really was the cutest thing.

"Are you about to laugh over the fact that I like hot cocoa?" She scrunched her face, and her little cheeks blushed.

"No, well, a little." He had the grace to duck his head and feel slightly ashamed. "It just sounded like something an elf would like to drink."

She blinked at him, threw her head back, and laughed. Relief flooded through him that she didn't hate him or anything over the fact that he had been rude.

"Yes, I guess that is an elf thing to drink. My hobby is baking cookies, just FYI. Oh, and I do giggle, own pointy shoes, can sing any Christmas carol that you've ever heard of and most that you have never heard of, I have a fabulous fruitcake recipe that even the most ardent Christmas hater would enjoy, and I'm great at giving gifts. Just don't ask me to wrap them. I hate wrapping."

He started laughing, and tears streamed down his face as he held his side. "Oh, God, I don't know why that's so funny."

She joined in his laughter, making him feel like less of an ass. "You just don't know any other elves, at least none that you know of. But don't freak out, I'll tell you everything you need to know."

When they settled down, he led her to his car and they drove toward the diner. Holiday was a small town with only one really decent place to eat—the town diner. Even though it should have been an old greasy spoon, it wasn't. The food was fabulous, and when his friend, Ally, was working, the company was nice.

They shuffled through the light dusting of snow and walked through the doors. He pointed out how empty it was. There wasn't a single other soul there except his brother, Matt, and Matt's fiancé, Jordan.

Matt raised an arm and called out. "Hey, Justin, come and join us; bring your friend." His little brother grinned, and Justin held back a groan. Great, as soon as someone saw him with Rina, the whole town would think he'd found a new girlfriend. Okay, maybe he did want to sleep with her and find out everything about her, but that did not make her his girlfriend.

Sure, keep telling yourself that.

He ignored that inner voice that sounded annoyingly like his brother Jackson and looked down at Rina. "Do you mind if we join them?"

"No, not at all. Actually, I think it's a great idea. Since there's really no one else here, we can talk freely. I think it would be a good idea if your family knew everything that's going on, especially since they've had dealings with the paranormal."

Justin looked at her and frowned. "How do you know that?"

She bit her lip and blushed. "The North Pole has a file on all executives and their families. I know it's intrusive, but they have to know what you're dealing with so they keep everything online. It is a business after all."

"I don't think I like the fact that you know so much about my family and me, and I know next to nothing about you."

"You can ask me anything you want, and I'll tell you. I know it's odd that I seem to know so much, but it's really just because of your job. It's magic, and they know a lot. I'll fill you in, and maybe you won't feel so nervous or whatever it is you're feeling."

He looked down at her big blue eyes and nodded. "Okay, let's go get something to eat, and then you can tell me what it is about my family and the supernaturals."

"Oh, it's not just your family. It's more like the whole town."

He froze. "Okay. You're going to explain what you just said to me in front of everyone."

He put his hand on the small of her back and guided her toward his brothers table. He didn't care about the knowing glance Matt gave him at the placement of his hand. He just really liked the feel of her small body pressed against his and the heat radiating from her. He liked it a little too much.

"Matt, Jordan, this is Rina." She gave a little wave, and Matt and Jordan nodded, clearly interested in finding out who the blonde at their brother's side was. "She's here to help me with... I guess a job that I have to do?"

"That sounds mysterious," Jordan said. "Take a seat. Ally is the only one here, so we have free rein of the place. That way you can tell me just what you are, Rina, dear." Jordan sounded protective of him and just a little too mean toward Rina for his taste. He wrapped a protective arm around Rina's shoulders, but she didn't move.

"I'm an elf, and thanks for being rude about it."

Jordan's eyes widened and she had the

grace to blush. "I'm sorry. I just didn't know what you were and why you're with Justin. I know I'm protective of him and his brothers, but that didn't mean I should ask like that. I'm just very momma-witch with the Cooper men."

"Uh-huh. Maybe next time just wait for someone to introduce herself. Oh, and don't worry, I know you're a witch."

Justin squeezed her shoulder as he watched the two of them go at it. "Okay, this isn't going as well as I'd hoped. But, let's just get it out in the open, shall we?"

The door opened, and Abby, one of his elementary teachers, and a friend of the Coopers, walked in. "Hey, I didn't know you guys would be here." She stopped halfway to the table and took in the scene. He knew what she was seeing, two couples sitting at a table. She was so painfully shy sometimes when it came to men that she really had no idea what it meant to be on a date, and he felt sorry for her. Not that he would ever say that to her.

"Join us, Abby; we're just meeting Justin's friend, Rina," Jordan said.

Just then, Ally, the diner's best waitress and another family friend, walked toward them from the back of the restaurant, a tray of waters in her hand. "I saw Abby drive up, so I got everyone water. If it's all right, I'm going to join you since I'm starving. I haven't had a chance to eat today. I know it's not usually appropriate, but no one's here and y'all are my friends." She set the last of the waters down, then bit her lip and looked around. "And I just invited myself to lunch. I'm sorry about that. I'm going to go to the back and crawl under the oven if that's okay with you." She tucked her tray under her arm and tried to step back.

Rina stood up quickly, and he immediately felt the loss of her heat next to him. This couldn't be good. "No, join us. I know you're all friends, and it's okay if you guys hear what I have to say. I think it concerns you all anyway." Abby and Ally frowned but walked closer.

"Okay," Ally said. "Why don't I get your food first and then I'll sit?"

Justin glanced at the menu and smiled. "How about you just get us all the stew, some of that crusty bread I know you make, and whatever soda you feel like. We're not picky."

"Sounds great to me," Matt said. "Can we help, Ally?"

She waved her hand and shook her head. "No, you can't go in the back. That's against the health code. I'll be back quickly. The stew is already made. All I have to do is serve it up."

While she did that, they all sat down in an awkward silence after introducing Rina to Abby. As soon as Ally came back with the stew, Matt stood up and helped her serve it, and then they ate and waited for someone to start.

"Okay, Rina, how about you start with why this whole paranormal thing is about the town rather than the Cooper family."

"What?" Matt asked.

"Well, Justin had said that something must be up with the Coopers, with what had happened to you, Matt, and the fact that you're now going to marry a witch. Oh, and the fact that Justin is one of Santa's executives."

"Santa's what?" Jordan asked.

Justin quickly explained that Christmas Eve night so long ago and the weird feelings he'd been having. "We'll get to exactly what that means for me in the future in a minute, but first I want her to finish talking about the town."

"Holiday, Montana, was given that name for a reason," Rina began.

"I thought it was because of Doc Holliday," Abby interrupted.

Rina shook her head. "No, it's actually because this town is a siphon of holiday supernaturals. You see, each of the holiday myths, which are assumed to have been contrived in order to make children happy, are actually based on real supernaturals and real events. So, there are leprechauns, cupids, and even elves. You already know about ghosts and witches, and there are a few more. But those things are drawn to Holiday. I don't know exactly why, I'm sure there's a reason, but all of those things are real, and over time, they like to congregate here."

"How come no one ever knew that?" Jordan asked as Justin just sat there and tried to take it all in.

"I'm not sure. Maybe people just forgot or didn't want to know. Even though people in this town know witches, and maybe even ghosts are real, it doesn't mean they want to believe it. Not many other people around the world really know the true reason behind holiday supernaturals and this town, so maybe something was lost over time."

"Okay, but how do I fit in?" Justin asked, still reeling over the fact that the world was much bigger than he had thought.

"You are going to be an executive for Santa," Rina answered. "Christmas is as much a business is anything. Yes, it is commercialized, but our business isn't about making money. It's about remaining magical and always having the same essence infused into the holiday even if no one wants to think of it. Your job will be spreading the Christmas cheer and goodwill to all children. Kids still believe in Santa, and that helps Santa keep his magic. Without his magic, he couldn't go to each house in every culture's home the world over and leave the presents."

"You're saying Santa is real?" Justin asked.

Rina let out at annoyed breath and gave a small growl. *Very cute.* "Yes, I thought it was understood by now that Santa is real and he does give gifts. However, most of the time, people don't realize it's him. Parents don't believe in Santa, so the magic allows the parents to think they were the one who bought the gifts that Santa brings. It's really annoying. You would think that the parents would just be okay with Santa and having help with the Christmas holidays, but no. They want to be the ones who give their child the favorite gift, so Santa lets parents believe that."

"You're telling me Santa has mind control powers?" Justin asked dryly.

Rina laughed, and the others at the table joined in. "I wouldn't call it that. If anything, you're going to be the one who has mind control powers."

"Huh? Like a superhero?" That would be cool. As long as he didn't have to wear the tights. That would not look good on him.

Rina snorted, and Matt threw a roll.

"Hey, no food fights. I don't want to have to clean up." Ally scowled.

"Sorry," Matt grumbled.

"No, not like a superhero," Rina said as she patted his hand. Tingles shot up Justin's arm, and he wanted to pull her closer. Not a good time for that, maybe later. "Your job is to be in charge of the district. I have the information back in my room, but with you being in town and helping where needed, the magic will pour out of you, and it will all work out. It's quite handy."

"Why can't Santa do that?" Justin asked, feeling like this was all too much.

"Because of the amount of kids and parents in the world. There's only one Santa. However, he has thousands of executives, and these executives have assistants that help. It's all an amazing system if everything works out. It's just someone dropped the ball and didn't train you. That's why I'm here."

Justin let out a breath "But what if I don't want to be an executive?"

"You don't have a choice."

"So, Santa gets cheap labor?"

"Your life isn't cheap, and you were an exception. Most people want to be one of Santa's executives. But I'll help you."

"Will I have to live at the North Pole?"

"No, your job is going to be to live here in your district. If you want to move, then it may take some shuffling with the other executives, but it does happen. You may have to go to the North Pole sometimes for meetings, but that's not very often."

"I just take a flight to the North Pole? Because that happens every day."

"No, you'll take a snow globe. That's how we travel. Each snow globe goes from one Santa-approved place to another. I'll show you how they work.

"Wow," Matt whispered, and he tugged Jordan closer. Abby and Ally looked to be in a trance with all the information being spread. They each knew about Jordan and what Matt had been, but this had to be a whole new thing for them. It sure was to him.

"I don't know if I can do this," Justin said.

"I'm here to help you."

"Because you're my assistant?"

She blinked then bit her lip. "No, you'll get an official assistant later." A guilty look spread over her face, and his disappointment grew. She was leaving? He wasn't gonna work with her? Why did that make him feel as though he were losing something he didn't even know he'd wanted? And why did Rina look so guilty?

Chapter 4

Rina stared at ceiling above her bed and held back a sigh. She didn't want to get out of bed. She was so warm and comfortable, but her job awaited. She winced. No, not her job, the job she'd stolen.

She was not really good at this whole bad-elf thing. Though the lunch with Justin and his family and friends had gone well, she still felt like a fraud.

She wasn't an assistant, not yet. She might know exactly what Justin needed to do and could make lists of how to help him succeed, but that didn't make it her right.

She didn't want Justin to get in trouble for something she had done.

She got out of bed and blushed, remembering the way Justin had touched her in small ways throughout the day. He'd led her through doors in two places, guiding her with his hand on the small of her back, and he'd repeatedly put his arm around her shoulders, whether it was for comfort or protection, as it had been with Jordan's scrutiny. She liked it oh-so-much every time. Each time he touched her, she'd wanted to sink into him, inhale his crisp scent, and close her eyes. Thankfully, she hadn't. That would've been embarrassing.

But, she couldn't keep on lying to him. It wasn't fair to anyone. She'd been selfish, stupid. With a new determination running through her veins, she quickly showered and got ready for her day. As soon as she tightened the last bit of her bun, she nodded at her reflection. A bittersweet feeling filled her. She might have been ready to help Justin, but her conscience wouldn't let her go. She needed to tell him everything, yet she couldn't. What if she lost him and the job? What if she hurt him? God, lying sucked. She wasn't going to do it again.

She walked down the stairs and into the small dining room of the inn. No one else was residing, and she felt as if she were a guest in Connie's home rather than in a public place.

"Well, hello, darling," Connie said with a bright smile as she walked into the room. "Good to see you up and about on a Sunday morning. Are you going to eat something before you head off to Justin's?"

Rina laughed. "You really are closer to a fairy godmother than an innkeeper. Are you going to get me some glass slippers?"

Connie snorted and set up Rina with a plate of pancakes and sausage. Rina's stomach rumbled, and she blushed. "Why would I get you glass slippers? They'd just pinch your feet and then you'd break them somehow and end up with bloody feet. Never made any sense to me why that girl had them. It must've been lost in the translation at some point."

Rina just shook her head and bit into the fluffy pancake. Oh, goodness, she was going to have to jog or something or she was going to gain a lot of weight. Like all people from the North Pole, she could have a lot of sugar and her waistline would still be okay, but this was getting ridiculous.

Rina finished up her breakfast just as her cell phone rang. Connie left the room with the dishes, giving Rina some privacy. Without bothering to look at the caller ID, she answered.

"Hello?"

"Rina?" a deep happy voice answered.

Oh. God. It was Santa. The Santa. Not that there was more than one or anything.

"Yes, Santa, it's me." God, she was going to be fired and lose everything she'd ever known. Why had she been so impulsive?

"I'm glad you recognize my voice. You know why I'm calling you, don't you, dear?"

She nodded, swallowing the fear down, and then remembered he couldn't actually see her. "Yes, I know. I'm sorry, Santa. I didn't mean to do something so impulsive. This is so unlike me. I don't know why I didn't, I mean... I'm sorry."

"I know you are, dear. We're going to talk about that in a minute, but first, let's talk about Justin as an executive. I didn't realize he didn't know anything. Everything in his paperwork said he knew. I don't know who wrote in that they told him, but I'm gonna find out that for sure. Justin is going to need you. I can't afford to let anyone else go down there and help him out, and I know you can do it. Don't think I haven't noticed the fact that you've been keeping up on what the assistants do. I know you are quite capable."

Then why haven't I been allowed to be an

*actual assistant? S*he bit her tongue before she actually said that aloud. It wasn't the time; it might never *be* the time.

"Rina, you shouldn't have run off. It wasn't very responsible of you, and we're going to have to talk about it when you get back, but now is not the time. I know you've been unhappy, Rina. Some things are going to have to change around here. I don't know what, but we'll figure it out. Just take care of Justin, and I'll take care of the rest later."

Was Santa really saying everything would be okay? Hope filled her, but she didn't say anything. She wasn't willing to break the mood and ruin it.

"Rina, the reason I'm calling you personally is because I wanted to let you know you are valued."

"Really?"

"Yes, I wish you'd known that. It's just that, for some reason, Jack wanted to keep you where you were. I know that man as if he was my own, but I don't understand why he would do that. It's something to think about, but not for you to worry about, dear. Do what you can with Justin, and then we'll figure out what to do about you and your happiness. Because you will have to be reprimanded in some fashion. I promise, though, it won't be too bad. You broke the rules, but without you, Justin would have been lost on the most important date of the year."

"I understand." But hope filled her anyway. Maybe she could be an assistant. Maybe even Justin's assistant. That meant she would be able to be near him...and there weren't any rules about romance...

Enough of that. It was so not the time.

"We need you to help Justin spread the goodwill of man and bring the idea of Christmas to the children who won't hear otherwise. Oh, they know the idea, but it's the executives that enhance it. The executives help keep the magic alive, and I'm going to need you to help Justin realize that."

"Oh, yes, I understand."

"Good, Rina. I have faith in you."

"Thank you, Santa," she whispered into the phone. They said their goodbyes and hung up.

Santa believed in her. Rina could do this. She could.

She quickly said goodbye to Connie then headed to Justin's place. Today would be their first day of training. Not just his, but hers as well. She wasn't hiding from the North Pole anymore. She was actually going to be acting like an assistant in the open. They would be going to an orphanage a couple hours from town, and she and Justin would be playing board games and helping them with lunch. All the while, she'd be helping Justin spread

Christmas cheer. An assistant wasn't just someone who helped with the paperwork. No, she would actually be helping him harness his magic and learn control. That is, once he learns to actually use it, but that would come with her help.

She'd also tell him the truth. Though Santa had told her she could stay, she didn't want to lie to Justin anymore; she couldn't.

The snow was just starting to fall as she pulled into Justin's driveway. She'd checked the weather earlier and known it might be a small storm or something bigger; it just depended on how fast the wind moved it through town. Hopefully, it wouldn't stick for longer than normal. Though her SUV could handle it, she wasn't in the mood to drive in a blizzard.

She tugged her hat down on her head, made sure her glamour was working, and got out of the car. The wind howled, and the cold bit at her. She hugged herself and made her way to the front door, which opened as soon as she hit the front step.

"Hey, get inside. It's got to be cold as hell out there," Justin called out as he gripped her elbow, leading her in. She tried to ignore the heat that spread from his touch.

It would be totally inappropriate to want him.

But, in reality, the connection between an

assistant and their executive could be an intimate one if they let it. They were sharing magic, and sometimes a connection would hold. She hadn't thought about that when she'd come down here. Honestly, she hadn't thought much of anything. But, she couldn't think of any of that now. No, she had work to do.

Plus, the object of her thoughts was staring at her with an intensity that threatened to send shivers of need down her body.

"Rina?" Justin's deep voice caught her attention, and she wanted to moan. Fruitcake, she had to get off that track. "What's wrong? Are you still cold?"

He pulled her closer and ran his hands up and down her arms. She almost closed her eyes and leaned into his touch but resisted. Barely.

"I'm fine, just warming up." She pulled back from his arms and tried to ignore the sudden loss. "Are you ready to go?"

Justin smiled, though she could see the tension on his face. "Sure. I've been to this orphanage before. I love working with kids, hence the reason I became a principal." His eyes widened, and his lips thinned. "Wait, did that happen because of what Santa did to me?"

"I don't know," she whispered. "It could have been because of the magic running through you, but honestly, I just think you're that good of a person."

He nodded, but she didn't know if he believed her. "Okay, are you ready to go?"

She watched as his jaw firmed, and she felt the urge to trace her fingers down his stubble. He hadn't shaved that morning, and it only made him look sexier. This was going to be a long day.

"Wait, before we go, I need to tell you something." She took a deep breath and steadied herself. She really didn't want to lose Justin right when she'd found him. Not that he wanted her or anything; it was just a job. Right.

Justin furrowed his brow and looked to her. "What is it? You look so serious. Are you okay?"

Oh great, he even looked all caring and compassionate.

"So... I didn't tell you the full truth before."

His lips thinned, but he didn't say anything merely nodded for her to continue.

"I'm actually not a real assistant." She bit her lip and rubbed her hands together then stopped. She needed to look cool and professional. That was the only way she could get through this. "I'm actually the list organizer."

"The list organizer. Like the 'naughty and

nice' one?"

"Yes, I take the old lists and organize them, so that way, we'll always have a database backup. I work in the basement of the workshop. I don't really get to see anyone. My job is also to call the executives about a month before just to check-in. But, even then, it's more of a hello and goodbye phone call, not really anything of substance. But, when you reacted the way you did, I saw a way to help you. I'm so sorry I lied to you. I feel terrible. I want you to know I know what to do. You can trust me about that. I know you probably can't trust me with anything else because I lied, but I will help you get through this. I even talked to Santa today, and he wants me to stay and help you. Please, I'm so sorry."

Justin was silent for so long that she didn't know what to do. Was she just supposed to leave because he was angry? Or, maybe stay and let him yell at her?

Please talk.

"I knew something was off."

She blinked. What did that mean?

He came up to her, and she held back a flinch. Justin was a good guy. He wouldn't hit her or anything, right?

He wrapped his arms around her and held

her close. She stiffened for a second then let her body do what it wanted to do. It relaxed into him. She inhaled a crisp scent that was just him and held back a sigh. He was so strong, so manly. Was it wrong that she just wanted to stay in his arms for just a little while longer? Like maybe twenty to thirty more years?

He didn't say anything for another few minutes; he just held her. Reluctantly, she pulled back so she could stare up at him.

"Justin, not that I don't like it, and that's not to say I *do* like it, but why are you hugging me?"

He looked down at her and smiled. "I just felt like doing it. Everything will be okay. I knew something was off when you looked so guilty yesterday. But, for some reason, I trust you. So, let's start off fresh, and you can tell me all about what I need to do today. Because I'm just a little bit nervous." He squeezed her, and she squeezed back. She could get used to this. Not that she would.

He pulled back and got his coat, looking embarrassed. Well, he could join her in the embarrassment category. She didn't think long hugs were a job requirement, but it sure was nice.

"I'll drive if that's okay," Justin said as he tugged her hat over her head. She didn't know why he did that, but she was starting to crave his touch. Not a good thing. "I know you live up at the North Pole, and all but I know these roads a little bit better."

"Okay, that's fine with me."

They shuffled out to the car, and he even opened the door for her, closing it after he made sure she'd settled in. As they drove toward the orphanage, Justin kept his eyes on the road, but kept the conversation up. They talked about their childhoods and his job as a principal. She could tell from the way he smiled and grew animated how much he loved his job, even if she knew that he somehow doubted his reasons for accepting the job in the first place.

When they got to the orphanage, all the kids stared at them, their eyes wide. Some looked as if they were happy to see new people while others shielded themselves, not wanting to get their hopes up. Luckily, the administrators had explained to the kids that Rina and Justin were just volunteers, not a couple looking to adopt. It broke her heart just thinking about these kids being alone on Christmas. Maybe through Justin, and even her help, they could experience a little more Christmas cheer. Christmas wasn't about having presents and getting material things. It was about finding happiness in the smallest of ways. That was Justin's job as the executive—to make sure that they could feel that special holiday joy.

"Okay," Justin whispered and leaned down to her. She could feel his warm breath on her neck, and she held back a shudder. This was neither the time nor the place to be thinking those thoughts, but what delicious thoughts they would be. "What do I need to do?"

She leaned closer to him so others couldn't hear. Yes, that was the only reason. "All you need to do is use the energy I know you're feeling at the edge of your fingertips and brushing along your skin and funnel it out. The magic knows what to do. You just need to be here."

"That's it?"

"You don't know how to control it yet, so that's what I'm here for." She took his hand and tangled their fingers, ignoring the way her pulse leapt at the touch. "Since I'm your assistant, I'll be your funnel. So just release what you can, and because I'm an elf, I can help you manage it. And it will feel weird, but I won't let you hurt anyone."

He pulled her back to a corner, his face grim. "I could hurt someone? Why didn't we practice before?"

She put her free hand on his chest and patted above his heart. "Because you need a large group of people who need cheer in order to start. I'll help you. And, you can never hurt anyone. It's more of the fact that you could spread too much happiness or energy, and things could go a little haywire, but that's why I'm here. I won't let anything happen to you or these children."

He looked down at her, and their gazes connected. Her heartbeat was so loud she could hear it drumming in her ears. "I trust you."

She let out a relieved sigh and pulled him toward the group of kids in the playroom. "Let's get started."

They kept their hands entwined as they listened to the kids talk, and they watched them play games. She could feel Justin's energy building within him, and she tugged on his hands. When his gaze met hers, she raised her brow, and he gave a little side smile that did annoying things to her insides.

With that, he released his energy, and she tightened her grip.

He was powerful.

Magic poured through her, and she funneled it toward the children. She could see the kids starting to pick up their shoulders, smile a bit, giggle, and play games with more interest. She turned her gaze to Justin and smiled. He looked so happy watching the children cheer up.

This was why an executive and his assistant were so important. This was why they were needed.

He continued to pour energy through her, and she could feel the connection taking root. It wasn't sexual, but heated, intimate, close.

Rina didn't know how she felt about that. On one hand, she loved it. Loved the way that she could feel him, the way she knew he must be able to feel her. On the other hand, it was like getting one touch of something you knew you wanted but probably could never have.

She was helping these children, and that meant she could be a true assistant. Could she be just an assistant? Not all assistants and executives were in romantic relationships, but in those cases, they weren't attracted to one another. Considering all assistants were male, and there weren't many female executives, the likelihood of a relationship forming was minimal, but from the way she and Justin kept looking at each other, she might be in for a world of heartache.

They stayed for a couple more hours and then left, leaving happier children than when they'd first arrived.

"That was amazing," Justin said as they got in the car and started on the way back to Holiday.

She smiled right back at him and bounced in her seat. "I know. I'm so happy just watching those kids. You did it, Justin. It was you and your magic."

He shook his head and took his hand off the steering wheel long enough to pat her knee. The tingles shot right up her body, and she bit her lip.

"You did most of it I think. All I did was

release that tension, but you took care of it, and you made sure it didn't hurt anyone or go wrong. You are the amazing one, Rina."

She blushed and shook her head. "Let's just say it was a team effort."

"Deal. Now, I am hungry. I know we fed the kids there, but I didn't feel comfortable eating their food since I wasn't starving. Want to go to the diner and get some lunch?"

She looked at him, surprised. "Really? You want to spend more time together? I'd have thought you would've grown tired of me."

"I don't think I could ever get tired of you, Rina. Let's go get some food."

She warmed at his comment but didn't say anything back. She wanted him, really wanted him. This couldn't end well.

Chapter 5

Justin walked the halls of his school, smiling down at the kids as they shuffled toward their classrooms. Some of the kids looked happy, enjoying their day and loving school. While the others looked like they'd rather be anywhere else, including playing out in the snow. His magic pulled within him and beat against his skin. He could feel it —like a magnet —reaching, longing to help the kids who weren't happy. When he'd used it for the first time with Rina at the orphanage, it was as if his body had decided it was time to stop being sluggish and instead be a full-time executive. He still wasn't sure if he was up to the job, or even wanted it, but, apparently, his magic—or whatever the hell they called it—was ready.

The school bell rang. The last of the kids shuffled to their classes, and the teachers closed their doors. He walked the empty hall, content that all was okay. He loved his job.

But, thinking about the fact that it might not have been his decision to go down this path made him pause and feel uneasy. Rina had told him that it might not have been Santa's interference that made him choose to be a teacher, and then later a principal, but he wasn't sure. He didn't remember the exact moment he'd decided to go into the teaching field, but he knew it was soon after the ice incident.

Did that mean, because of someone else's interference, everything he had done from that point on wasn't by his own choice? He didn't know how he felt about that. It was as if his life was out of his hands and someone else was taking control.

There was nothing he could do about it now. He loved what he did, even if it was a product of an accident. And, now, thanks to Rina, he had another outlet to help children and figure out who he was.

Rina.

He'd felt the way her pulse increased every time he touched her. He'd known then it wasn't just him. Thank God. He loved the way her smile brightened every time something good happened.

Had he just said love in connection with a woman?

He needed to slow the hell down. He hadn't even kissed her yet. Oh, he had been thinking about it. A lot. Like every thirty seconds or so. And not just kissing. No, he wanted to know what her skin tasted like. She smelled of sugar cookies and cinnamon, and he wanted to see if her skin tasted the same. Now he knew why he'd been craving sugar cookies like a maniac. Because, apparently, he was Santa's minion. Well, whatever the happy equivalent of that was. But, damn, he really wanted to know what Rina tasted like.

He knew she was his assistant, and he probably shouldn't be thinking those types of thoughts about her, but he couldn't help himself. She just fit so right against him. He hadn't meant to hold her so close the day before, but he was glad he had. She had tucked close to him and held on tight. He had only wanted to comfort her so she knew that everything would be okay. She'd looked so distraught at doing something so impulsive.

For some reason, he couldn't fault her for it. He knew there was more to the story than her being stuck in the basement of the workshop, and he needed to figure out what it was. Maybe in time she would trust him enough to tell him, and then maybe more

More what?

More of her? To be with her? To taste her?

He didn't know, but he wanted to find out.

He walked to the end of the hall to his office and closed the door behind him. He was at work, and it wasn't the greatest time to be thinking about a sexy little elf he wanted to get to know a little bit more. Okay, a lot more. He worked on more of the budget and all the messages that had accumulated from parents and city officials until the bell rang again and it was time for the students' lunch break. He would take his later.

He walked to the lunchroom and watched the kids file through the lines and sit down at their appropriate tables. Most were happy and energetic as they ate and talked with their friends, but some were little more laid-back and even sad. The urge to help them and shore them up overrode everything else, and he let out a bit of magic.

What could it hurt?

Without Rina by his side helping him to control it, it burst from his body with no control. Some of the children's eyes widened, and their smiles brightened. They started talking faster and grew perkier, and others looked like they had so much energy they couldn't sit still.

Then the first piece of Jell-O flew across the room.

"Food fight!" a fifth grader yelled from his table.

It was chaos with food flying in every direction. Teachers yelled at them to quit, getting hit in the face and arms with food for their efforts. Every single kid joined in, their lunches forgotten in terms of food and now thought of as weapons. They pelted each other, laughing and giggling, their energy increasing so much they gave him a headache.

He quickly damped down his energy, closing it off before he did any more real damage. Some of the kids immediately sat back down, their excess energy depleted, and their behavior returned to normal. For others, it took a little bit longer until they sat down.

Justin looked down at the pot roast currently sliding down his shirt and sighed. This was all his fault. He needed Rina to help him. He'd done too much, and he didn't know what he was doing. He'd put these people in danger because he thought he was better than he was. What if someone got hurt because of him? He would never be able to forgive himself.

The teachers looked to him for guidance, and he gave them each a nod.

"I trust this won't happen again," he said calmly, his voice low and deep. The students quickly nodded, their mouths shut, their eyes wide. With that, he turned on his heel and walked out the door. He trusted his teachers to take care of it then follow the food fight disciplinary guidelines. Each student involved had to clean up part of the mess, meaning the next class would be disrupted. But, it would teach them manners and a sense of responsibility. What about his own responsibility?

It had been his fault, after all.

Justin shut himself in his office, changed into a clean shirt, and sat down on his little futon in the corner of his office. He rested his head in his hands and tried to fight down the nausea that threatened to take hold. He'd let go of too much energy at once, and now he was shaking. He knew his face was pale and clammy, and he was glad no one could see him.

Cowardly, he spent the rest of the day in his office and went through his numerous piles of work. The teachers came in one by one to let him know that everything was handled and the children were properly sorry. Each teacher remarked that the children said they had no idea what had come over them and even said that the teachers themselves had felt like they wanted to join in, it had been so energetic. Justin merely shook his head and said the fact that they'd cleaned it up was punishment enough; they didn't need to lose recess or anything else. When the final bell rang, he needed to get out of there. He packed up and watched the kids get on their buses and load into cars as parents picked them up.

He was a failure, an epic failure. He would have to tell Rina what he'd done; it was only fair. She had told him her mistake, and he would have to tell her his.

He waved and said goodbye to some of the students as he made his way to his car.

"Oh, Justin, I mean Mr. Cooper," a voice purred behind him and then giggled. He resisted the urge to vomit. He hated to hear giggling, except for when Rina did it. For some reason he didn't mind Rina's giggle, but the woman behind him made him want to tear off his ears then gouge out his eyes with a wooden spoon so it would leave splinters.

He turned as he put his fake smile on. He was in public and couldn't actually slap the woman, not that he would.

"Hello, Mrs. Booth, I see you're here to pick up Dustin."

She waved her fingers and let out another giggle, and he clenched his jaw at the pain of the sound. "Oh, what do I keep telling you, Mr. Cooper? Call me Cindy, please." She batted eyelashes that had way too much clunky mascara on them and came up to him with her arms outstretched. "I heard about what Dustin participated in today at lunch, and believe you me; I will take care of it when I get home. I just wanted to let you know that I do take care of everything in my possession." She winked then reached around and grabbed his ass.

Seriously?

Justin pulled back, anger running through his veins. "Make sure you get Dustin home okay in this weather, Mrs. Booth." He narrowed his eyes, and she stepped back, her face losing a little bit of that blush. Good. "The weatherman said it's going to start snowing a little bit heavier tonight, so I would just make sure you get home ahead of that." He leaned closer to her so her son, who looked embarrassed, wouldn't be able to hear. "And, if you ever touch me like that again, I'll make sure that your husband gets Dustin in the divorce."

He turned away, got in his car, and drove off before she could utter a word. He was so pissed off that the woman had the audacity to grab his ass in public. Not to mention the fact that she was fucking married and her son was standing right by her. He did not understand some of the moms at his school. They were ridiculous and scornful. He might be one of the youngest principals around, but that didn't make him an open meat market for them. He took a deep breath trying to calm himself and drove directly to the inn. He didn't even bother going home to change out of his clothes. He just needed to see Rina. He tried to tell himself it was for work, but even he didn't believe that. Justin wanted to see her because he knew as soon as he was in her presence she would lighten up his day.

He pulled up to the inn, got out, and walked in without knocking. He knew Connie liked to think of it as a home rather than a public place to the town residents, but he needed to see Rina now.

He walked directly to her room, knowing she was the only guest at the inn, and knocked. When he heard her soft voice saying come in, his tension eased just a little bit. It was amazing that just her voice could do that.

Her eyes widened, and she smiled when she saw it was him. "Hi. I didn't know you were getting off work so early. It's good to see you."

Without thinking, he pulled her into a hug and rested his cheek on her head. She stiffened for only a moment then wrapped her arms around his waist. He inhaled her sweet, sugary scent and let out a breath.

Her soft laugh tickled his chest, even through the layers he wore, and he squeezed a little harder. "Did you have a bad day at work?"

For some reason he could imagine her

saying that on a daily basis when he walked into his home and she would stand there, asking him how his day went like a real couple.

He pulled back and brushed a curl behind her ear. "Yeah, I guess you could say that."

"Is there anything you want to talk about?"

He loosened his tie, took off his jacket, and made himself at home in her room. When she sat down at the edge of the bed, he purposely sat down in the armchair. That way he wouldn't succumb to the need to lay her down on the bed just to see what she tasted like.

"I did something really stupid today, and then when I was leaving, I had an incident that I don't even want to get into."

Her eyes widened, and she scooted closer so that she could take his hands. He covered her small hand with his big ones and squeezed.

"What happened today? I want to hear both things because you look like you need to talk."

"Yeah, I guess I do." He missed talking with people about his day. Yeah, he had his brothers, but they didn't live with him, and he had been feeling lonely. He just didn't want to get too dependent on Rina in case she didn't feel the same way.

"Then tell me. That's what I'm here for, to listen." She smiled, and her big blue eyes twinkled.

"Well, we'll start with the thing that wasn't my fault. On my way out of the school, I was accosted by a mother."

She frowned. "What did you mean by accosted?"

He cleared his throat, uncomfortable. Maybe he shouldn't have started with this one. "Uh, she well, she grabbed my ass. In front of her son. Oh, and I forgot to mention, she's married."

Rina's eyes narrowed, and she gave a cute little growl. "She did what? How did she think in any way that was appropriate? Especially in front of her son. Peppermint balls! That poor kid. Not to mention you. Are you okay?"

"Peppermint balls?" He smiled. Damn, she was so cute.

She blushed all the way up to her ears. "It's just how I curse. Don't make fun of me. You didn't answer my question. Are you okay? Did she hurt you?"

Justin laughed, feeling better already. "Look at you worrying about the mean old lady trying to hurt me. I can take care of myself; it just pissed me off. She didn't hurt me, don't worry."

"Well, if you want, I can go and take care of that for you." She smiled devilishly, and he laughed.

"I would pay to see that."

"Okay, now I think you're making fun of me."

"Never."

"Uh-huh. Why don't we just leave that subject now, and you can tell me about that thing you did that *was* your fault. If you're saving it for last, it must be something big."

He closed his eyes so that he wouldn't see the disappointment when he told her. He didn't think he could face that. "I was having a good day until I went to the lunchroom and had all those kids around me. I did something stupid."

"What?"

"I let my magic out, trying to cheer them up, and I let out too much and didn't control it. They got so rambunctious they had a food fight. They could've gotten hurt because of something I did. I shouldn't have done that. I should've waited for you. What the hell was I thinking?"

He kept his eyes closed, but she still held onto his hands. Her touch was the only thing keeping him together.

"Justin, stop beating yourself up. Yes, you should've waited for me. No one got hurt, so think of the good things. With more practice, we can teach you control. You're just going to have to learn and to not use your magic when it's not needed.

You don't have to unleash it when we're not working."

"What does that mean?" He finally opened his eyes and relaxed, and he didn't see any disappointment in her gaze, only calm understanding.

"I told you before that each region carries an executive. That executive doesn't meet every child, doesn't have to help every child. Just the fact that they are there lets their magic work. The only reason that you would need to unleash your magic is if you're in a place or position, where it would be helpful. Just the fact that you were in that room would have helped the mood or just kept the magic alive. If you ever find yourself needing to get rid of an excess, find me. That's what I'm here for."

For some reason the thought of releasing his tension with her made him think dirty things and not what he should have been thinking of. Their gazes locked, and she blushed. Yep, she was thinking the exact same things.

"Tell me more about yourself."

She blinked and frowned. "What do you want to know?"

"I want to know about you and your family. I just want to know more. You said you'd tell me since you know so much about my life and I know next to nothing about yours."

"Oh, well, what do you want to know exactly?"

He rubbed small circles on her wrist and smiled. "Any brothers and sisters?"

"No, I'm an only child. Most elves are since we don't really have a lot of space to move around. Only assistants really get to move from the North Pole."

"Really? That doesn't seem fair."

"Oh, no, we like it. Well, I mean most always do. Elves love their workshop at the North Pole, and they don't want to move, but it isn't like we're trapped up there."

He tilted his head, sensing an undercurrent in her words. "What about you? Did you feel trapped? Is that why you came here without being told to?"

She bit her lip and nodded. "I never really liked my job, and I know that makes me a bad elf. But I like working with you, so maybe I did find something for me."

He traced her jaw and loved the way she shivered. "I'm glad I'm helping you too." He moved his finger up her jaw again and traced her ear, and she froze. "What? What did I do?"

"You didn't do anything. It's just my ears are a little sensitive." She blushed, and he held back a groan as his cock hardened.

"Oh, really, why is that?"

"You can't really see because I have my glamour on, but elf ears are pointed, and it's sort of an erogenous zone for us."

"Really?" He smiled and leaned down closer to her so that way their noses touched.

"Show me," he whispered.

She pulled back ever so slightly, her breath quickening. "Okay."

He watched as her glamour fell, and her pointed ears appeared. He never would've thought he would've found them sexy, but hot damn. Since she'd said they were an erogenous zone, he couldn't wait to trace them with his tongue.

His gaze locked with hers as he traced the tip of her ear with his finger. She shuddered, and he smiled.

Fuck yeah.

With their eyes still on each other, he leaned down and brushed his lips against hers. They were so soft, plump. She moaned against him and closed her eyes. He traced the seam of her lips with his tongue, and she opened for him.

Yes.

He framed her face with his hands and deepened the kiss, his tongue touching hers, their mouths moving with each other. It was the sweetest of kisses. She moaned again, and he nipped at her lip. He kissed her harder, and she pulled back.

"Damn, I loved that." There was that love word again.

"That can't happen again," she whispered.

He blinked, not understanding exactly what she'd just said. "Why?"

"Because you're just getting to know me, and it might just be the magic that's making you do that. I don't want it to interfere with anything." She looked down at her hands, and he just wanted to pick her up and hold her close. She looked so unsure of herself, and he felt like he was the cause.

"We're going to do that again, Rina. The only magic that happened was the magic between us, not anything having to do with what we are."

"You should go."

He traced her ear again, and she shivered. "We will talk about this."

"I don't know, Justin."

He didn't say anything else, just walked out the door. He didn't want her for just one night, but for a whole lot more. He was attracted to her and could see them being together for more than just a one night stand. He wanted to see her smile and laugh and be in his arms. He even pictured her round with his child.

He froze and almost fell down the stairs.

What the hell? Where'd that come from? Why the hell was he thinking about babies?

Not any babies. Rina's babies.

For some reason that didn't scare him at all. Now he just had to get Rina on the same page as him. He smiled and walked out of the inn toward his car. Yes, he'd enjoy getting her to see his side. He already liked her more than he'd known just that morning. He couldn't wait to see when she realized she was his.

Chapter 6

It had been almost five days since Justin had kissed her, and Rina still couldn't get it out of her head. His lips had been so soft, softer then she had expected. She loved how tentative it had been at first, and then the kisses had grown into something more passionate. She almost could have surrendered to him right then, but she couldn't. Though she had imagined it every delicious way, the real thing had blown her dreams out of the water. She didn't pull back at the first touch of his lips, but didn't sink into him not wanting to melt against him or, worse, throw her arms around him and ride him like a pony. Because that would've been bad.

Very, very bad.

Imagining that she was doing just that fluttered across her brain, and she groaned. Even though she hadn't wanted him to leave, she was glad that he had. Yes, he was sexy and funny and seemed to actually like her, but she couldn't give into those feelings. He had a job to do and so did she.

She was an elf who didn't even know what she was going to do with the rest of her life. She didn't even know if she had a job when she went back to the North Pole. She could only stay in Holiday if she remained Justin's assistant, and that wasn't even close to being a true possibility.

Rina stood up and shook her head. She needed to quit wallowing and get some work done. Because she was a list organizer, she was really good at making her own lists. Even though Justin's magic was inherent, that didn't mean he didn't have work to do. She already had made a list of the places he could visit, and now she needed to add it to the schedule and include training exercises for when they could connect again and use his magic.

Her body warmed at the thought of that connection, but she shook it off. No, she couldn't think like that.

A knock at the door pulled her out of her thoughts. She looked down at her watch and frowned. Who could that be? It couldn't be Justin; he was still at work. She quickly piled everything and hid the important things in case it was someone who didn't know the magical nature of the town. She could never be too careful.

When she opened the door, she froze. Oh, no, it couldn't be.

"Hello, Rina, dear," Jack Frost sneered as he walked through her open door, uninvited. "I'm surprised you had the gall to sneak out and disobey my direct orders. Who do you think you are, Rina, dear?"

Rina blinked and tried to gather the courage to talk, but she couldn't. She never could stand up for herself against Jack. He scared her more than anything else in the world. The fact that he was her boss made everything that much worse.

She stared up at his gray eyes with their ice fractures. If they hadn't looked as if they held the devil within them, they would've been beautiful. As it was, they looked as if they could see into her soul and steal it. His white-blond hair was perfectly coiffed, a strand never out of place. The chiseled features looked as if they had been carved from stone. He looked to be the perfect angel, yet she knew what lurked underneath the mask was anything but.

She balled her fists and straightened her shoulders. Santa had given her the okay. She wasn't in trouble anymore, except with Jack. "Santa called and said I should stay on as Justin's assistant, at least for this season. You didn't have any reason to come here, Jack."

Jack strode to her, his pristine suit looking as though a speck of lint wouldn't dare to touch him. She held back a shiver of revulsion and as he traced her jaw with his finger.

"I have every right, Rina, and you know that. You snuck away without saying anything to your dear old boss, me. Santa may be the figurehead, but you know I am the one to pull the strings. I'm the one you have to answer to."

No, that wasn't right. Santa, or Kris Kringle, as he was known to others, was the boss. He was the one who made all the decisions, and Jack was only his second-in-command. Wasn't that right?

Jack traced her ear then he moved his hand back to grip her hair around the bun. He pulled, and she winced.

"You don't get to do anything without me. Don't you understand that? You're lucky I don't send you back to the North Pole to live in that pitiful basement where you'll never see anyone you love again and be all alone without anything. Your parents won't even talk to you if I have anything to do with it. You are just an elf. A nothing. You belong on the bottom of my shoe, not here in Holiday acting as if you know what the hell you're doing."

She raised her chin, and he pulled her hair harder, breaking the elastic. Her hair fell in ringlets to brush the top of her ass, and he smiled.

"You are a beautiful woman, Rina."

She bit her tongue so she wouldn't say anything that could land her in a world of trouble. Jack had more magical powers than most and could kill her in an instant if he felt like it. She was only a conduit and would be powerless against him. Fear clawed at her stomach, and she closed her eyes.

She needed to get out of there, now.

"Rina, like I said before, you should not have left. You're lucky that I'm going to be generous and let you stay here. It's so sad that that Justin fellow slipped through the cracks. I wonder how that happened."

What did Jack have to do with it? The way he said it made her think that Jack had done something that meant Justin would fail. An untrained executive was a dangerous thing. Their magic could get out of control like it had in the cafeteria with the food fight. People could be hurt, and the people who desperately needed some holiday cheer might not get it. What had Jack been trying to accomplish?

"I'm here now, Jack." She was surprised at how steady her voice was. Go her. "I'm here to help Justin, and everything will be okay."

Jack released her hair and smiled a cool smile. "Oh, I know everything will be okay. Because I'm going to stay in town and make sure you know how to do your job."

Alarm spread through her. No, he couldn't stay. "But what about the workshop? Don't you need to be there to oversee everything?"

"I can do that from here, Rina. You forget I know all and see all. I'm Jack Frost after all." He turned from her and walked toward her little desk in the corner where her work was sitting. "I see you've been busy, dear. But, remember, you still need to be punished for what you did. You can't just leave without telling me. That old man can easily forgive you because he doesn't know you. But, I know you, Rina. I know that you are merely a lowly elf who deserves to be in the basement. You're nothing, Rina. You better remember that."

She took a couple steps toward him without thinking, and he snarled.

"You shouldn't have left. You should have

left well enough alone. And now you will pay."

His eyes glowed with a frightening, icy white stare, and the room grew colder. It was so cold, she could see her breath. Icicles frosted along the window.

Jack Frost wasn't just Santa's second, but the man behind the actual legend of Jack Frost. With the flick of a wrist and the thought of an icy tundra, he could freeze anything in his path and create ice by just the water molecules in the air. He could freeze the water inside the human body and kill a person within seconds. She wrapped her arms around herself as her body shivered, her lips going numb, most likely blue.

He reached down to the desk and grabbed her folder with all the work she'd been working so hard on.

"You don't need this, do you, darling?" He smiled again, and ice ran down his arm and spread to her folder. When a thick sheen covered the entire folder and its contents, he threw it against the wall. It shattered into a thousand pieces, and she bit her lip so she wouldn't cry out. All her work, gone.

"Don't you ever disobey my rules again, do you understand, little elf?"

She nodded, unable to speak; her lungs were so cold.

SANTA'S EXECUTIVE

"You're lucky I don't make it worse for you, dear." He flicked a piece of ice off his shoulder then straightened his body as the room warmed around her. Her body sagged as blood rushed to her extremities.

The room went back to normal as if nothing had happened, and Jack stalked toward her again. He gripped her hair in his fist and pulled.

"I'll be watching you and that little Cooper. Step a toe out of line, either of you, and you'll wish I had frozen you now." He pulled back then straightened his suit again while she tightened her grip on her waist.

Why couldn't he just leave? He'd scared her and destroyed all her work. Wasn't that enough?

Another knock at the door startled her, and she froze again.

Please, don't let Jack hurt whoever it is.

"Why don't you answer the door, darling?" Jack said, his eyes twinkling with something she didn't want to think about.

She walked to the door, straightening her outfit as she did. Though the room was warmed, she didn't want to scare whoever was on the other side of the door. When she opened it, she let out a sigh of relief that quickly turned to fear.

"Justin!"

"Rina," Justin said as he smiled. His blue eyes gazed at her. She wanted to jump into his arms and feel like nothing bad could happen. Yet, she also wanted to turn away and have him run the opposite direction so Jack couldn't harm him. She wouldn't be able to live with herself if anything happened to Justin because of her.

Justin looked behind her and frowned. "I'm sorry. I didn't realize you had company." His voice lacked emotion, and she missed the warmth. His warmth.

"Oh, sorry. This is, um, my boss, Jack." She waved her hand toward Jack while Justin moved closer to her in the room. It was as if the room had gotten smaller with the addition of just one more person. She wanted to grab Justin and run, never looking back at any of the responsibilities and dangers that they faced. She was more responsible than that, at least slightly so.

Jack smiled again then walked toward them, holding his hand out. Rita didn't think Jack would do anything to Justin right now, but she couldn't be too sure. She watched as they gripped hands for a strong shake and moved away from each other. She held back a sigh of relief when Justin looked as if he hadn't been hurt from it.

Small favors.

"So, I guess that makes you my boss as well?" Justin asked as he stood slightly in front of

Rina as if sensing the danger from the tension-filled undercurrents.

"I'm afraid not. Elves are the only things under me."

Rina winced at the derogatory and innuendo-filled comment but didn't say anything back. She hated being the weakling in this situation, but antagonizing him would only make things worse.

"I see," Justin said, but she didn't think he did. Why wouldn't Jack leave so that way everything would be better?

"I'm just here to make sure Rina doesn't need help. Because, as you know, she's not very experienced in this. I wouldn't want anything to happen to her, or to you."

Justin nodded and brushed her arm with his hand, as if trying to calm her. She winced as Jack caught the movement. Peppermint balls, this couldn't be good.

"Well, I'll be staying at the inn as well, just to make sure everything's okay. It was good to meet you, Justin." Jack walked out the door, closing it softly behind him, and Rina let out a sigh.

Immediately, Justin pulled her into a tight hug and ran his hands up and down her back. He kissed her forehead then traced her lips with his thumb. She sank into him and closed her eyes. This felt right, but it couldn't be.

"What was that? What's going on?" Justin asked as he ran his hands through her hair. She would have purred in contentment, but she barely held that back. His hands felt much different from Jack's. Strong, yet soothing and gentle.

"It's nothing." She didn't want to worry him, but she could tell he didn't believe her.

He tapped the tip of her nose with his finger then kissed it. Butterflies flew around her stomach, and she blushed.

"Don't lie to me, Rina. I thought we were in this together. What did Jack want, and why does it look like you were scared to death of him?"

"He's just my boss."

"Rina, you can trust me. I need you on my side in order to get through this, but I also want to be by your side to get through what you need to get through. Let me help."

Reluctantly, she pulled away from him and sat on the edge of her bed. He quickly sat right next to her and wrapped his arm around her shoulders.

"He's the basis for the legend of Jack Frost."

"Seriously? So, he forms ice and cold and

the winter?"

"I don't think he actually forms winter. I think that is an actual weather phenomenon. But, he can form ice, and he can make the room colder."

"Did he hurt you?" Justin growled, and Rina felt all warm inside. He looked damn sexy when he was being possessive. Who knew she liked alpha cavemen?

"No, he just wanted to warn me."

"I don't think I like you staying here."

"Justin, I'll be fine."

"No, you're going to stay with me."

Lots of naked breakfasts and sweaty nights filled her mind, and she shook them away. That was why they couldn't sleep under the same roof. She wouldn't be able to trust herself.

"I'm going to be fine. Jack won't hurt me." Well, that was a lie.

"No, you're going to stay with me."

"But, what about Connie?"

"I'll talk with her to make sure she stays at her daughter's house. Jack can fend for himself here because I don't trust him. You know I'm right. You can stay in the guest room and everything. You can trust me."

"I know I can." She didn't trust herself.

"Then stay with me. We can train together and get to know each other better. Please."

She let out a sigh and ignored all the voices in her head saying how much of a horrible idea this would be. She didn't feel safe with Jack around, and even though it made her feel like a stupid woman, she wanted Justin around. Safety in numbers, and all that. Yes, that was what she was going to stick with.

"Okay."

Justin smiled and kissed her softly. "Good."

"But, no kissing."

"Sorry, you already agreed before you tacked that on. Don't worry. I'll behave myself. Mostly." He grinned and stood up. "I'm gonna go talk to Connie, and I want you to stay in this room. Don't open the door unless you hear my voice. We'll take both cars and head to my place now. So, pack up."

He ran out the door, closing it behind him, and she lay back down on the bed. What the hell was she getting herself into?

She quickly packed up her meager belongings, ignoring the sight of the now-thawed pieces of her notebook. Justin came back up to her room within minutes, and then they left to go to his place. He set her up in the guest room, and she felt a pang of longing that she wouldn't be in his room. Jeez, she needed a nice long nap. Her emotions and thoughts were all over the place.

Justin came in behind her and wrapped his arms around her waist. Without thinking, she leaned back into his embrace.

"How about we make dinner and watch a movie? What do you say, roomie?"

All she wanted to do was jump into bed and sleep wrapped in Justin's arms, but there was nothing else to say except "That sounds great."

They made chicken Alfredo, laughing in the mounting sexual tension in the kitchen. Then they piled onto the couch and ate while watching a cheesy romantic comedy. After their bellies were full, Justin pulled her into his arms again, and they cuddled on the couch.

She burrowed into his side and told herself it was only for the night. The only reason she was letting this happen was because Jack had scared her earlier, okay, always. Tomorrow, they would act professional and be friends. She was his assistant, nothing more, but as Justin traced circles on her shoulder and she could hear his heartbeat under her ear, all she could think about was how perfect this was and how she wanted more. Restraining herself might prove even more dangerous than Jack.

Chapter 7

"I can't wait until Jordan takes up her spot as the mayor," Abby said then she banged her head against the desk. "I'm so tired of still having to do everything according to the board's old ways. Lesson plans suck."

Justin threw his head back and laughed. "I love how you filter it when telling me how you really feel about lesson plans. I am your boss, you know."

Abby blushed and rolled her eyes before getting back to the tedious job of making sure the lesson plans were not only approved by every state and national guideline, but also to the ignorant and outdated guidelines of Holiday. Oh, the laws for their town were perfect for their time, but it had been a hundred years, it was time for a change. Justin hated them, but luckily their old mayor, a corrupted, black-hearted man, was in jail for a very long time for trying to kill Matt and Jordan. And soon, his sister-in-law to be, Jordan, was going to be the new mayor, so things were about to change.

"Just think, this may be the last semester we have to worry about rules that were put in place over a hundred years ago," Justin said as he picked up a sugar cookie. He bit into the soft, sugary delight, frosting coating his tongue. Jesus, he was losing it. At least he had an idea of why he was craving sugar cookies every day. Though he may have to try to hold himself back at some point, he didn't want to actually look like Santa.

"True. It would be nice to be able to teach without having to imagine a horse-drawn buggy taking the kids to the one-room school." Abby laughed as she took a cookie. Justin ignored the urge to take it back from her. He really needed to stop acting as if he was five.

"These cookies are so good, Justin. I cannot

believe you can bake. You Cooper brothers keep surprising me." Abby closed her eyes and moaned as she bit into the cookie, and Justin just shook his head. He was pretty sure he looked exactly like she did when he bit into one, so he couldn't fault her for that.

They worked another hour, eating way too many cookies but getting everything done they needed to.

"Jeez, Justin, how did you let me eat all those cookies?" She stood and patted her already generous hips and sighed. "It's a wonder you're not gonna have to roll me out of here."

"Oh, shut it, Abby. You're beautiful, and you know it."

She blushed then rolled her eyes. He'd said it before to her, but she never thought he was telling the truth. Though neither of them had feelings for the other past being good friends, he still thought she was one of the most beautiful and nicest people he'd ever met. It pissed him off to no end that Tyler couldn't see that. It was as if a curtain stood between Tyler and Abby. No matter how bright she shown, Tyler was blind to see it. Maybe once Justin figured out his own love life, he'd be able to help Ty with his.

"Hello? Justin?" Rina's voice echoed from down the hall, and Justin smiled.

"We're in here, Rina!" Justin called back then started to clean up so he could go home with her. Her SUV hadn't started that morning for some reason, so she'd dropped him off at work. It felt so domestic and it surprised him he enjoyed it. He didn't want to think too hard about what that meant.

"Look at that smile on you," Abby said as she helped him clean. "So, the rumors must be true."

Justin blushed and felt like a giggling schoolgirl. "I'm not going to gossip with you."

"Ah, but that's no fun."

"Oh, I'm interrupting," Rina said from the doorway, her eyes wide. "I can go wait out in the car if you want, Justin."

There was something in her voice that made Justin pause. He looked back down at what she was seeing, and he silently cursed. Abby was bent over the table, cleaning up things, and he was bent right beside her, though from Rina's point of view, it probably looked a little more risqué. Crap.

He quickly stood up and put on his coat. "No, were done."

"I see."

No, he didn't think Rina saw what was really happening. He would have to fix that. "Come on,

Abby, we'll walk you out."

Rina didn't say anything but smiled at both of them as they walked silently and awkwardly down the corridor. He risked a glance at Abby, but she shook her head and widened her eyes. Yeah, he probably shouldn't be looking at her if he wanted to prove to Rina that there was nothing going on.

They said goodbye to Abby and piled into Justin's car. Rina didn't say anything but was still smiling, as if she couldn't quite not be cheerful. Maybe that was the elf in her.

"You do realize that nothing's going on between me and Abby, right?"

Rita looked at him and shook her head. "It didn't look that way to me."

Justin reached out and traced her jaw with his finger, her skin soft beneath his. "We were just cleaning up because I was excited to go home with you. Abby is in love with Tyler."

"Oh."

"I wouldn't have kissed you and offered to let you stay with me in my home if I was with anyone else. I like you, Rina. I want to be with you." He leaned over and pressed his lips softly to hers. She stiffened for only a moment then relaxed, parting her mouth ever so slightly. He took the invitation and brushed his tongue against hers. She let out a little moan, and he deepened the kiss, their breaths quickening. He pulled back reluctantly and traced his fingers along both of her ears. She shuddered and bit her lip.

"Considering we're in my school parking lot, we should probably go home and finish this there if that's what we're going to do."

"Are we?"

He groaned and shifted in his seat, his cock rubbing against his zipper. "Let's get you home."

"I'd like that."

He swallowed hard and visions filled his head, mostly of her naked beneath him as he licked every inch of her skin to see if she tasted like sugar. Damn, he needed to get a grip on his control if he wanted to drive home safely. As it was, the ice on the roads would require all of his attention. His cock might be demanding he sink into the sexy elf beside him, but he was stronger than that. Maybe.

He drove carefully down the icy roads, doing his best not to look at Rina. If he did, he might lose control of the car or pull over to taste her again. Jesus, he was acting like a teenager again. He hadn't had sex in his car since he was sixteen, and now, at thirty-four, all he could think about was gripping Rina's waist and pounding into her.

"Justin? Are you okay? You're groaning, and

your knuckles are white from gripping the steering wheel. Are the roads that bad?"

She placed her hand on his thigh, and he held his breath. Jesus, she felt like heaven.

He was going to have to go for honesty here because if he lied and blamed it on the weather she might do something dangerous and rub his thigh. His cock perked up at that. Bastard. "I'm fine," he croaked out. "The roads aren't that bad. I just need to get my mind off of doing really dirty things to you and I'll be fine."

"Oh," she said on a breath, and then from the corner of his eye, he saw her look down at her hand and pull it away quickly. "Sorry."

"Don't be. I love you touching me, but unless you want me to pull over right now, let's wait the next two minutes of driving to get home, okay?"

"Okay."

They pulled up to his home, and he turned off the car, his body not relaxing in the slightest. Jesus, what were they doing? Were they going to jump on each other the moment they walked in? Was that what she wanted? Damn, they were going to have to talk.

Rina opened her door and shuffled to the house, and he followed right behind her. He watched as her short dress hugged her ass, and he barely held back the urge to grip it in his hands and bend her over the porch railing. It was a bit too cold for that, and he didn't think his dick would like the outdoors in this weather. Plus, they needed to talk. Yeah, that.

They got into the house, took off their coats, and stood awkwardly in the foyer.

"So," Rina said as she bit her lip.

Damn, he wanted to be the one to bite her lip. No, he had to get his priorities straight.

"I think we should talk," he blurted out. *Oh, yeah, smooth, Romeo.*

"Oh, okay." Her voice sounded so dejected that he wanted to kick himself.

He made it to her in two strides and framed her face in his hands. "I want you, Rina. So bad it hurts." She pulled back a bit and looked down at his cock straining his pants, and he let out a hollow laugh. "Yes, that hurts, too, but I was talking about the fact that it hurts here." He released her face and pressed her hand to his chest above his heart. Her eyes widened, and he let out a deep breath.

"Why would you hurt there?" she whispered.

"Because every time I look at you, I see more. I don't understand it, Rina. I hardly know you, and we're both working at a new thing in our lives, and it's crazy. But, I want you, Rina. I like the thought of you in my home, under my roof. Last night, when you were in the guest room, so close to me that it would only take a few short steps to have you in my arms, I couldn't sleep. I don't just want you so I can make love to you. I want you for more than that, but I don't know what."

He'd never been so open and honest with anyone in his life, and he was freaking himself out. Why did he want this woman? Yes, she was beautiful and kind, but he'd never wanted to think about a home with another woman. What was it about Rina, and why was it moving so fast?

She pulled back from him, and he grew cold.

Fuck.

He'd opened himself up, and she was going to reject him. He fisted his hands and tried to seal off his heart again.

"Justin..."

"No, it's okay. I'm sorry I said anything. I'm going to make hot chocolate before dinner. You want anything?" He turned from her, unable to look at the woman who was about to take his heart and not want it or worse, tear it into shreds.

"Justin, wait. Let me talk." She placed her hand on his elbow, and he stopped and turned toward her, unable to move any farther. What was it about this woman that made him crazy?

"What is it, Rina?"

"I like you, Justin. I really do."

"I'm sorry I made you uncomfortable."

"Oh, shut up! Let me talk."

He widened his eyes and smiled. He loved when she got feisty. "Okay."

"That's not shutting up."

He closed his mouth and tried not to smile again. He failed.

"I like you, Justin," she repeated. "I like you too much I think. No, don't speak yet," she added when he opened his mouth. "I know everything is crazy with Jack and your new job, but we can figure that out. What we can't figure out is what I'm going to do, Justin. I may not be your assistant forever. Don't you understand that? I'll have to move to back to the North Pole. I don't want to start anything that could break us. I'm not strong enough for that."

The thought of her leaving sent ice through his veins. No, she couldn't leave. Not when he'd just found her. She'd settled too deep within him for him to be able to let go. It might have been just the residual of the magic running through their veins, but if so, that was just the beginning. He loved the way she laughed, the way she took charge, the way he could picture her in his—no, their—future. He wanted her. Needed her.

He took the last step toward her and rubbed his hands down her arms. "I don't want you to go."

She sighed and leaned to rest her head against his chest. "I don't want to go either."

"Then don't."

"I may not have a choice, Justin."

"Then we'll make it a choice. If you can't be my assistant, we'll find you something here."

She looked up at him, her big blue eyes pleading. "Then I would be hiding who I am."

God, he didn't want her to do that. It would kill her just as much as it would kill him to see her go. "But, if you go back, you'd be back in a place you hated, at least if you go back to the job in the basement. Could you do that?"

"No, I couldn't, but I don't know what to do, Justin. Everything is up in the air, and it's scaring me. I hate not knowing."

He leaned down and kissed her softly. "Then let's work on what we *can* fix. We can make sure you're the best damn assistant out there so you can stay. Then we can make sure we're happy. I want you, Rina, and I don't want to watch you go. I want you in my bed, and I want you in my life."

She shuddered and hugged him tighter. "One step at a time?"

"One step at a time."

"Then what's our first step?"

He ran his hand down her back and cupped her ass. Her eyes widened, and her breath caught.

"I can think of a few things."

She blushed and kissed his jaw. "Oh, yeah, like what?"

"Hmm." He kissed the tip of her ear as he kneaded her ass, rocking into her as he did so. His cock was hard against her belly, and he groaned. "I've been wanting to taste you since I first saw you. I want to run my tongue along every inch of your skin until you groan and plead for more. Then I want to fill you slowly until you're clawing at me to move. Then I want to wrap your legs around my waist and pound into you until you call my name."

Her breath had gone ragged, and her eyes had dilated as he'd spoken his wants. She gripped him tighter and nodded.

"I want all of that, and then we can do more."

He grinned and kissed her temple. "Hell,

yeah."

"And all of our troubles will be still be there when we're done."

He kissed her other temple and led her to his bedroom. "Yes, but we'll figure them out. I won't let you go without a fight."

"Why do we want each other so quickly, Justin? It doesn't make any sense. I thought people were supposed to slowly burn, not ignite as quickly as a match."

He turned toward her and unzipped the back of her dress as he gazed into her eyes. He let her stand there without disrobing her further as he tried to come up with the words that needed to be said.

"I don't know, Rina. All I know is that I want you for more than a night. I was attracted to you from the start, even when I wanted to get you out of Jackson's home. I don't understand it. I always thought things like this were supposed to take time."

He didn't tell her he loved her because he wasn't sure he did. He didn't know what that feeling felt like, as he'd only felt it for his family, not a woman. He knew he might well be heading toward there, though he didn't tell her that. He'd already scared the both of them enough for the night. Now, he wanted to get her naked so he could taste her.

Yes, that sounded like a plan.

"One step at a time, right?"

"Right." He lowered his lips to hers and drank her in. She tasted of sugar and sweetness, everything he wanted. He slowly stripped her out of her dress and pulled back to look his fill.

Fuck.

She stood in only a forest-green lacy bra and matching panties with green stockings that ended in lace at the top of her thighs. Her breasts were high and full, and he knew they would overflow his hands perfectly. Her hips flared out and begged for his grip. She wasn't a toothpick; no, she was perfect. A woman. His woman.

His gaze trailed up and down her body until he reached her face. She blinked, looking uncertain. Damn, he wasn't doing his job if she didn't feel like he wanted to bend her over and fuck her right now.

"You're beautiful."

She blushed, and he kissed her neck, trailing his lips down her collarbone.

"I want you."

"Good, then have me."

He groaned and knelt in front of her, kissing her body along the way. "I want to taste you."

Her whole body blushed, and she ran her hand through his hair. "You don't have to do that."

He looked up to her and grinned. "Oh, yes, I do." Slowly, he took off her panties, keeping her stockings on. He froze as he bared her pussy to his gaze.

"Damn."

She squirmed, and he slowly turned her so she could sit on the bed. "I've never done this before."

"Good. Then I'll be your first." *Your only.* "Lie down. Let me love you." Neither commented on the use of the L-word, but it was just as well. He wanted—no, needed—to taste her, now. She did as he asked, and he spread her thighs with his hands. He felt her tense beneath his palms, and he squeezed. "Relax, baby."

"I trust you."

He warmed at her words. God, he wanted her. He licked his lips as he gazed at her core, wet and pink. His. Oh, yes, his. He traced the outer lips with his finger, and she wiggled.

"Stop moving, baby."

"But, I want you. Let me touch you."

"You'll get me." He circled her clit then touched her core, loving the way she responded and tightened for him. He lowered his head, flicking his tongue against her warmth as she groaned his name. Good.

He licked her again, this time savoring her sweetness. Fuck, he could dine on her for days. He sucked and licked her as she pressed herself against his face, seeking more. Greedy wench, he loved it. He continued to taste her until he felt that telltale tightening, and she came, screaming his name and causing him to almost come in his pants.

Fuck, she was beautiful.

His.

Who knew he could be so alpha? As she came down from her high, he quickly took off his clothes and sheathed himself in a condom. He wanted to taste those breasts of hers and knew he wouldn't be coherent enough to take care of protection later.

"Justin," she breathed, her eyes wide, dark with lust.

"I'm here, baby. You're so fucking beautiful."

"Let me touch you," she repeated.

He shook his head then rolled down her stockings. As much as we wanted to go slow and sexy with those, he couldn't wait any longer.

"If you touch me, I'll explode."

"Oh," she said as she smiled.

"Minx, you know what you do to me."

"I do now, and I like it."

"Good, I like it, too." He leaned over her and kissed her soundly, loving the way her tastes mingled. He unclasped the front of her bra and quickly got her out of it. Her breasts fell heavy against her, and he rubbed both nipples in his hands. They were stiff, rosy points on full breasts that begged for his mouth. He licked and sucked them as she thrashed against him. The bud tightened in his mouth as he bit harder. She rolled her body flush against him and he nibbled again.

"Justin, please."

"Oh, yes. I can't wait any longer." He gripped her hips and pressed the head of his cock against her opening. He met her gaze and fell that much more in love with her. This was the woman he wanted, needed. He held back a jerk as the thought settled in.

He loved her. Holy shit. He blinked but didn't say anything, not wanting to let the word take anything from him, from them.

Slowly, oh so slowly, he pushed into her, her inner walls clinging to him. She was so tight. Fuck. He kept going until he was fully seated within her, their breaths syncing, their eyes never straying from each other.

Then, he moved.

He thrust in and out of her, increasing his speed with each movement. She gripped his arms, and he moved so he could lean down over her, his forearms resting by her head. She trailed her hands up and down his sweat-slicked back, and he kissed her, his hips moving, feeling her tight around him.

"Justin..." Her eyes widened, and then he watched as she came, her pussy fluttering around his cock. The pressure pushed him over the edge, his seed filling the condom, and he yelled her name.

He laid above her, his cock still deep within her, and watched as she came down from her high. They didn't speak, merely looked at each other as if they both knew their lovemaking had been different. Yes, lovemaking, not just sex.

Special.

Perfect.

Theirs.

Now, Justin had to figure out what they were going to do about it.

Chapter 8

Rina snuggled into the warm body pressed to her back and sighed in contentment. Even after a week of sleeping in Justin's arms, Rina couldn't believe it had happened. She loved the feel of him behind her, holding her close. In his sleep, he ran a hand up and down her stomach until he finally rested and cupped her breast. Her nipple pebbled in his hand, and she bit her lip, so she wouldn't wake him.

As much as she wanted to lean into his touch then ride him like a pony, she couldn't. He hadn't been sleeping well. No, not because he'd been up all night making love to her—okay, maybe that was partially it, but not all of it. He'd been so stressed at work that he was working long hours and the tension bled into his dreams. With Christmas coming up so quickly, Justin now practically had two full-time jobs.

The school was in a state of ordered chaos. In a matter of days, the semester would end and Justin would finally be able to take a break. He'd been busy dealing with last-minute lesson plans and budget issues, as well as the day-to-day issues of being a principal in a town where he was the authority figure for most children. Every time there was a scuffle, an argument, or a child who just wouldn't listen, Justin would deal with it in stride. She'd stopped by some days to pick him up for their training, where she'd help him funnel his magic safely, and she'd watch the way, even though he was being stern, he still knelt down on the level with the kids and talked to them calmly. He never yelled, never threatened. He genuinely liked kids.

He would make a great father.

Rina stiffened and tried to control her erratic heartbeat. Where had that thought come from? No, she couldn't think like that. She didn't know whether this was going to be temporary or not. Even though Justin had professed his feelings, at least some of them, she still didn't know where they were in terms of their relationship.

She wanted to be with him so much. To be his assistant, to be his partner, to be his everything. With such far-fetched goals, she tried not to even think about it by living one day at a time. Something the list maker in her hated.

"Rina?" a sleepy voice asked behind her as Justin kneaded her breast.

"I would hope it was me considering what you're doing right now with your hand." She gasped as he pinched her nipple and rolled his rock-hard erection into her ass.

"True. But I was mostly wondering what you are thinking about and what has you so stressed and stiff."

She sighed and arched her back, grinding into him. "Speaking of stiff."

"You're insatiable, you know that?"

"Only with you."

"Good."

He lifted her leg and slowly entered her from behind, his cock filling her completely. They both lay still when he was fully seated, her body growing accustomed to him. Leisurely, he thrust in and out of her, playing with her nipples and trailing kisses down her neck. Her hips met him thrust for thrust, her body growing warm and tingly. He slowly trailed a hand down to where they joined and ran circles over her clit. She threw her head back and screamed his name as her body came in a lightning-quick spark of energy and need.

Justin followed soon after then held her hips close to his so she could feel his cock twitch within her.

"I could wake up like that every morning," Justin whispered then bit her ear lobe.

The feeling of contentment filled her again as she thought of forever. Ignoring the little seeds of doubt that weren't so little anymore, she turned her head and captured his lips in a soft kiss. "Me, too."

"Good."

"Wait? What about a condom?" she asked, fear and a little excitement flowing through her.

"Shit."

"It's okay, I'm on birth control and I can't get human diseases."

Justin relaxed and kissed her neck. "Thank God. I can't wait to be bare in you again."

She smiled, loving the feeling of just him within her.

They lay there for a few more minutes until she finally had to deal with nature. She quickly squirmed out of the bed, Justin's now-soft cock leaving her. When she came back, she found Justin sitting up on the bed, his back resting against the headboard.

"So, what do we have planned for today?" Justin asked as she purposefully sat at the other end of the bed so she wouldn't snuggle near him. They had things to do today, and if she touched him, they weren't going to be getting out of bed anytime soon.

"I know it's your day off from school, but not so much from your other job."

Justin closed his eyes and leaned his head against the headboard. "This seven-days-a-week work thing is going to kill me."

Rina bit her lip and reached over to pat his hand. She wasn't going to touch anything else if they wanted to get out of there. "You're in training. That's why it feels like you're doing so much. Plus, your body is still adjusting to the fact that you have so much more magic now that needs to release, so we need to figure out what to do with that. I know it sucks, but it will be better. Plus, school is almost out, and that means you can focus on being an executive for a bit. Then, after the holidays, you can take a little break before starting school again. After Christmas, the new job with Santa won't feel as big. It will just be something that you do subconsciously, something that I can help you with."

Justin opened his eyes and smiled at her, his blue eyes twinkling, the lock of black hair falling over his forehead begging her fingers to brush it away.

"I like the fact... no, I *love* the fact that you're thinking about my future with you by my side."

She blushed and ducked her head. She hadn't quite meant to place herself in that future. The bed moved as Justin got up and crawled toward her, and then he put his finger below her chin, raising her gaze to meet his.

"Rina, I like you thinking of me as more than just a holiday retreat. I can't explain it, but ever since I saw you, I just keep thinking about my future with you. Maybe we're moving way too fast, but I really don't care. I'll do what I have to in order to make sure you stay by my side. I just hope you want to be there."

"I want to be there," she whispered.

Justin smiled then leaned down and took her lips in a heated kiss. "I glad to hear that, baby. Now, what is it that you have planned for us to do today? I know you have lists of your lists. Let's get cracking so I can come home and unwrap you like a Christmas present."

Her body tingled at the thought of Justin undressing her and tasting her, and she blinked. "Enough of that. If you keep talking in that deep, sexy voice of yours we're never going to get anything done. And, before you say you don't want to get anything done, remember that this is for the children, and not for you."

Justin let out a putout sigh then laughed. "Fine, anything for the children."

She reached over and grabbed a pillow to smack him with it. "You are a dork."

"Yes, but I'm your dork."

"That was really cheesy."

"Just wait until you meet the rest of the family at Christmas dinner. I'm going to be cheesy in public."

She froze at the thought of being included at the Cooper dinner. "What?"

"You're my girlfriend, and I want you to be with me and my family on Christmas." He lowered his brows and frowned. "Was that too presumptuous? Did you want to go spend Christmas with your parents? I mean, I've never been to the North Pole, so I can spend the holidays there, I guess. I think my family would understand."

She smiled, leaned over, and kissed him softly. "It just surprised me that you wanted me to be included in that. My family will be with the rest of the elves at a huge event at the North Pole. You're welcome to come and join me up there, though you'll be the tallest one there by a long shot." She grinned, and he chuckled. "But, I think this year I'd rather be with you and the Coopers. I don't really know them that well."

"We're gonna have to change that now, aren't we?"

"Okay, now that we have Christmas Day plans out of the way, let's plan the rest of today since that comes first."

"You're a smart one."

She hit him with a pillow again. "Ass."

"I thought you liked my ass," he teased.

"Yes, I love your ass, but that is beside the point. Now, we're going to go to the children's Christmas play. I know the school doesn't run this one, but we're still going to go and make sure the kids are okay and infuse cheer when we can."

He leaned over and kissed her again, and she leaned into his touch just for a moment. She was only human after all. Okay, she was an elf, but she still had no control when it came to Justin sometimes.

"Then let's go take a shower and get ready to go." Still naked, he stood up and pulled her into his arms, his cock hard again and pressing into her stomach.

"Oh, no, I don't think so. We need to take separate showers and get ready so we actually get out of the house on time." He stuck out his lip and pouted. "That is so not a sexy look on you."

"Fine, I'll go wash my own back, but I blame you for this." He pointed down to his cock, which twitched at her attention, and she laughed.

"I thought I'd taken care of that today. Not my fault you get hard just by thinking."

"Hey, I'm not just thinking of anything. I'm thinking of you."

"Aww, that's sweet, but I'm still not going to have sex with you this morning. We're going to be late."

"You're mean when we have things to do."

"You better get used to it."

"Oh, I plan on it." He grinned then strode confidently toward the bathroom. She narrowed her eyes as he flexed his ass, taunting her. Darn man, he knew how much she loved every single muscle on him.

By the time they'd showered and made it to the Christmas play, the activities surrounding it were already in full swing. She glared at Justin, but he merely shrugged it off and smiled at her. He knew exactly what his smile did to her, and that was dangerous.

The play was an outdoor play with the pond and skating rink right next to it. People were bundled up, and most held paper cups of hot cocoa or coffee in their hands. Though it was cold, the wind had died down and the heaters were in place to keep everyone relatively warm. The children had wanted to have real snow for their play, so this year the adults had permitted the play to be held outdoors. By the looks of the rosy cheeks and cold faces in the crowd, she doubted the event would be held outdoors again in years to come.

"I see you two finally decided to grace us with your presence," Jack sneered as he walked toward them, his suit in pristine shape and totally out of place in the small Montana town.

Rina wanted to do the cowardly thing and hide behind Justin, but she was stronger than that. She had to be. "We're here, Jack, don't worry."

"It's my job to worry. Especially when I have an uneducated, well *you,* and in charge of something far greater than anything you could even imagine."

She narrowed her eyes and shut her mouth. Jack could take everything that she ever wanted away from her so she had to make sure she didn't antagonize him.

"Rina is doing a great job in helping me out. Know when to back off, Jack," Justin growled.

"Justin," Rina whispered.

"No, dear, let the man speak," Jack said. "He is, after all, your superior. You can't tell him what to do."

"She can say whatever she wants, but in this case, I'm a gonna tell you to back off. We can handle it; your interference is only that. Interference."

Jack narrowed his gaze, and Rina gripped Justin's hand. Her lover didn't quite understand the powers that Jack held, and she didn't want to endanger anyone, especially the children. Even though he was Santa's second-in-command, she'd still heard the rumors about what he could do from the other elves. She looked around and bit her lip. There were starting to gain attention, something that she wanted nothing to do with.

"I'm sure we'll be okay, Jack. Thank you for your concern," she said stiffly.

Jack glared, but he didn't say anything else. Justin gave a nod, and then led Rina away from what could escalate into a more heated confrontation.

"I don't know what that guy has against you, but he's really pissing me off," Justin growled.

She rubbed his arm and leaned her head against his shoulder as they walked. "I don't know either; he's just mean."

Justin looked down at her and narrowed his eyes. "He wanted you, didn't he?"

She stopped where she was and blinked. "How did you know that?" Her pulse increased, and she bit her lip.

Justin lowered his head until their foreheads touched. "I didn't know until you just said that. I was only shooting in the dark. He has the look of a scorned lover."

"I never went out with him."

"No, but he wanted to, and that's why he's acting like an egomaniac. Next time, tell me everything so I know what I'm getting into."

"I didn't even think about it. I mean it was so long ago and not even important to me. He's always been a bully. I just thought it was that."

He kissed her softly, and she noticed the glares of some of the women. It seemed she wasn't the only one with past issues, but that wasn't a surprise. Justin was a gorgeous man, and she didn't fault any of those women for wanting him. They just had to make sure they didn't touch him. He was hers.

He threaded their fingers together, and they walked toward the group of children getting ready for their play. They were dressed up in various Christmas and holiday costumes. There was a Santa, some elves—who looked nothing like her, but she wasn't going to say anything—a few reindeer, a snowflake, a snowman, even Jack Frost. Jack had to be getting a kick out of that. This play wasn't a religious one, but consisted of all the fantasy and myth that had to do with the holidays. Oh, she was going to love it.

She could feel the tension radiating through Justin as he gripped her hand harder. Of all the people around, and all the Christmas cheer that was slipping through their systems, she knew that Justin needed to release some of the energy and help even more. Their gazes locked, and she smiled. He gave a nod, and she could feel him let go. The energy slowly built through her, and she released it slowly. The small children who hadn't been smiling at the time lifted their gazes and grinned. The adults in the audience, who looked as if they wanted to be anywhere else but here, started to smile and quiet down as they got ready for the play. It was working. Justin was going to make a great executive.

Rina slowly funneled his magic and watched as the Christmas cheer did its job. She loved the holidays and everything to do with them. She might have been resentful when she was at the North Pole in her basement job, but that didn't mean she didn't love Christmas. Her connection to Justin solidified and strengthened. He looked down at her and smiled, squeezing her hand. She squeezed back and leaned into him. Their magic molded, connected, and intensified.

It was as if they were meant for each other. In all the warm and cuddly ways possible.

As soon as she thought that, a coldness spread through her limbs, and her lungs seized. She tried to remove her hand from Justin's, to break the connection, but she couldn't. Justin looked down at her, his lips turning blue.

Jack.

He was doing this, mutating their connection, their magic.

She tried to breathe, but couldn't, and her body shook. She leaned against Justin, and he leaned against her. She could feel him trying to cut off his magic, but neither could. Instead of the warmth and happiness that had been flowing through them, there was ice and loneliness. A child cried, and a parent ran to help but failed to reach them, sliding on the ice that formed beneath their feet. People started to scream, frantically trying to reach their children, not knowing why the sudden need had entered their minds.

Rina looked through the crowd, trying to find Jack. She finally spotted him on the other side, his hands outstretched, a snarl on his face. Why was he doing this? He was going to hurt these children. She tried to break down the magic again, but it was no use. Jack was controlling them. The screams intensified as she looked up and noticed icicles forming on the railings. The sharp ice fell, fracturing on the ground in thousands of pieces. People started to run away, but the ice was too slippery. Her body was cold, her labored breath coming in short pants.

She felt Justin's muscles tense beside her, and then he fell to his knees. Their entwined hands pulled her to the ground beside him as her body shook.

"Justin, we need to stop this," she said, her voice shaking.

"I'm trying," he grunted.

Instead of trying to break the connection with Justin, she focused on breaking the connection with Jack. She closed her eyes and imagined the ice that was attacking his system then warmed it with the thoughts of Justin and the Coopers. If she couldn't fight with the strength to break it, she could fight with the strength of love and warmth.

She thought harder and harder even as the screams intensified and the wind howled. She focused all of her energy on that icy connection and groaned. It had to work. It had to. Subtly, the connection snapped, and she could hear Jack scream across the crowd.

As quick as it had come, the ugly energy was gone. She collapsed against Justin, as they both were now able to clamp down on their magic. The ice melted away beneath people's feet, and she watched as parents gathered their children up and took them away, not knowing who to blame for this chaotic, freak storm.

"He could have killed them," Justin whispered as he pulled her onto her feet.

"I know; he's dangerous."

"We have to tell Santa."

"I know, but I don't know if he'll believe me. It's too busy right now. It's not as if I have a direct line to Santa."

"Try. We have to. We can't let this happen again."

She leaned into his hold and kissed his cold jaw. "I love you."

He looked into her eyes, and he captured her lips and kissed them, warming her to the bone. "I love you, too."

SANTA'S EXECUTIVE

Chapter 9

Justin slammed the cabinet closed and cursed. Jack could have killed all of those kids and their parents yesterday. Fucking Jack and his fucking problem with Rina. He didn't know what the exact issue was, but Justin needed to figure out. It couldn't all be because of a rejection. He didn't think Jack was that shallow, but he could be wrong. There had to be another reason that Jack wanted to cause so much destruction and death.

Justin's hands shook at the thought. He couldn't control his magic. It'd floated through him and through Rina at such an alarming rate, it had scared him. It scared him more than the fact that his body had grown so cold so quickly, that his lips had turned blue and his lungs had seized. What scared him more than that was the fact that Rina had been in distress right by his side, and he had no power over it. What was the use of having all this magic if he was unable to help the one person who he loved the most?

Jesus, he was a failure, again. It seemed that no matter how hard he tried, he couldn't shake the fact that he was nothing. A useless, bad boy who just fucked up everything in his path. He cursed again, having finally found the creamer he had been looking for. He poured some into his coffee cup and took a sip. He narrowed his eyes as the coffee burned his tongue.

Perfect. Just fucking, peachy perfect.

He poured some creamer into Rina's cup and added three times the amount of sugar he used. Even though he had a sweet tooth, even more so lately, his little elf loved sugar to a frightening degree. She told him she was an elf and it was just the way she was built. The amount of sugar used at the North Pole must be jaw-dropping.

He blew on his cup and took another sip of

his coffee, this time avoiding burning his tongue. He'd known from the incident in the cafeteria that his powers could go haywire and he would be a dangerous threat, but seeing the way that his powers had morphed into something he couldn't even comprehend had scared him. Nobody knew exactly what had caused the freak ice storm in the town square, but he always would. Even if the town never pointed a finger his way and never judged him the way that they had judged his sister-in-law, Jordan, for being a witch, he would always know that he had been responsible.

He didn't know how he was going to fix this though. Rina had told him Jack was stronger, having more powers than anything she or he could do. So, no matter what he did, he would not be able to win against Jack. They had tried to call the North Pole, but no one had wanted to talk to Rina. Apparently, they had called her a traitor, or at least someone who didn't follow the rules enough to be cared about. Rina had withdrawn into herself and hadn't spoken to him much since that call. So now, other than feeling like a failure about his own powers, he felt like one for not being able to protect her from the people who wanted to hurt her most. All Rina wanted to do was fit in and be worth something, and people were trying to take that away from her. He would do what he could to make sure she felt needed with him and within this town, but he didn't know if that would be enough. He didn't know much of anything anymore.

"Justin? What's wrong?" Rina asked as she walked into the kitchen, freshly showered and put together.

He leaned forward and kissed her softly then handed her the coffee. "Just thinking."

"Yeah, but it's what you're thinking about that worries me." She stood on her tiptoes and traced her finger down his nose. "Your face is all scrunched up, and you're frowning. That means whatever you're thinking about isn't good. Do you want to share?"

He lifted the corner of his mouth and shrugged. "Just the usual, stressful things, but I think I like the way that you can read my face."

She smiled then kissed his jaw. "I can't help it; your emotions are right on your face."

"Most people wouldn't think that. If anything, your face is more expressive."

"Well, that's true. I can't lie to save my life, but I can read your face, and I know something's troubling you. Tell me."

He let out a breath and set their coffee cups down on the counter. With his hands free, he pulled her into a hug and let her rest against his chest. She felt so right there, so perfect. "It's my fault that those people were in danger yesterday."

"No, no. It was Jack's."

"Yeah? Well, he used us to do it, so it's just as much my fault."

"That's my fault, too."

He frowned and kissed her forehead. "No, it wasn't your magic."

She huffed a breath and punched him softly in the side. "Okay, if you're going to blame yourself for Jack's mistakes, you can't just automatically think it's not my fault too. You make no sense."

"I'm angry. I don't have to be rational."

"Spoken like a true man." She grinned when she said it, and he leaned down to nibble on her lip.

"Stop trying to make me feel better. I'm in the mood to wallow."

She fluttered her eyelashes at him and grinned. "Sorry, no can do. Abby called earlier and wants to go ice-skating. Allison is taking her kids, and we're going to join them."

Fear slid through him, and he shook his head. "I don't think I want to be around people today, Rina. What if I hurt them?"

Rina ran her hands up and down his chest then wrapped them around his waist, squeezing hard. "You can't lock yourself away because of one person. Yes, he's dangerous. But, I figured out how to stop him before. We can do it again."

Yes, she'd told him how she thought of warmth and tried to sever the connection. If it worked that time, he hoped it would work again. Now that he knew that, he would do his best to help next time, if there was a next time. He hoped there wasn't.

"You sure you want to risk it?" Jesus, he sounded like some beta male. "You know what? No, don't answer that. Of course you want to risk it. Because you have a spine, and, apparently, I've lost mine somewhere." Frustrated with himself, he kissed her again then walked to the front door to put on his boots. "I take it you don't have skates, right? We'll have to stop by the store and pick some up for you."

He glanced up as Rina's body was shaking, holding back laughter. "What?"

"You're so cute when you're frustrated."

"I'm not cute; I'm manly."

"Oh, yes, you are that, but still cute."

"You know you'll have to pay for that," he growled, feeling better already.

She raised a brow and smirked. "There's no time for that. We have to stop by the store, get my skates, and then meet the girls and the kids."

It all sounded so domestic, and Justin loved it. He was learning more and more about her as the days passed and loved every bit of her. He wanted her in his life for as long as possible, forever if they could. That thought didn't scare him as much as it should have. It seemed the Cooper men were falling one by one, and he was okay with that.

They quickly got bundled up and headed to the store to pick up her skates. The general store in town had everything they could possibly want or need. Luckily, Rina's feet were small enough that they fit in the average-sized woman skate with thick socks. They purchased her skates and headed down to the outdoor ice rink on the outskirts of town. It was an old lake that, in the summer, was a popular fishing hole and a place where people went to swim. In the winter, the lake iced perfectly to skate on. Justin had come here with his brothers for makeshift games of hockey, skating, or just roughhousing. He loved it. He hadn't told Rina about it, but he figured Abby or Allison had mentioned the fact that all the Cooper men, except maybe Jackson who never really liked anything, loved skating.

As soon as the kids got out of the car, Allison's three children ran up to them. Ally was a widow who worked hard to provide for her kids, but he knew times were tough. If only she and his brother, Brayden, would talk to each other about their feelings, maybe some things would change in her life.

"Justin! You're here!" Lacy, Allison's

youngest at six, called to him as she threw herself into his arms. He caught her and nuzzled his nose into her neck. She giggled and squirmed and told him to let her down.

He'd always loved children, but seeing these three always made him want to have children of his own. He risked a glance over at Rina, and her rosy cheeks and bright eyes made him want to just lean over and kiss her. Jesus, his brain was moving too fast for him sometimes. He could already picture her round with his child. He quickly shook his head then knelt down in the snow to Lacy's level, her brown pigtails sticking out beneath her hat. Her big green eyes stared up at him with adoration.

"Well, hello there, Miss Malone. I hear we're going skating today."

She bounced up and down and bit her lip. "I'm getting much better at it, but will you help me?" She lowered her head but kept her gaze on him, giving him the cutest little expression ever. Oh, this girl was gonna be trouble when she got older. He glanced up at Allison and saw her roll her eyes. Yeah, Ally knew it, too.

"Of course, Lacy, hon."

"Yay!" She ran back to her mother, and Ally started to laugh.

"She has you wrapped around her finger, you know," Allison said as she sat down on a nearby bench and started to put on Lacy's skates.

"It's okay; I don't mind."

Cameron, Allison's middle child, came up to him next and grinned. "I can skate by myself, but I can help you with Lacy if you want."

Justin ran a hand through Cameron's shaggy brown hair. "Sounds like a deal, but I would put your hat on before your mom notices."

The little boy blushed and quickly did so. Justin looked over at Allison, who just smiled her thanks.

Aiden, Allison's oldest, came up to him next but didn't smile. The kid didn't smile often, and Justin thought it was because he felt like he had to be the man of the house. Hopefully, the Coopers would help him with that.

"Thanks for helping out my brother and sister," Aiden said, and then he grinned, surprising Justin. "You know, if you're going to be busy with them, I can help your lady over there."

Justin threw his head back and laughed, Abby, Allison, and Rina joining him. "You're a lady killer, are ya, son?"

Aiden held up his hands but was laughing with them. "Hey, I was just offering my assistance."

"You're twelve, remember that," Allison

called from the bench as she was tying up her own skates.

"Just trying to be helpful," Aiden said then walked over to another bench to start putting on his and Cameron's skates.

When they were all ready, Lacy gripped his hand and gripped Rina's on the other side. Justin met her gaze and smiled. Yeah, this felt right.

Cameron ended up holding Allison's hand while Aiden skated next to Abby. They laughed, skated, and tried to race each other as the morning waned and the temperature started to rise slightly. Rina took Lacy across the ice in slight circles, causing the little girl to giggle with glee. Allison and Abby sat on the side of the ice rink and watched, with Allison taking pictures. The boys skated circles around Justin, trying to one up each other. No one else was at the ice rink at that time, so they enjoyed having the ring all to themselves. They were just starting to get a bit tired and head in when Justin heard a sound like a gunshot.

He pulled Cameron and Aiden into his sides and froze. He looked around but didn't see anything then almost screamed. Another sound like a gunshot ricocheted across the ice, and Allison screamed for them to come in. He looked down and cursed. Cameron clung to the side as Aiden gripped his hand. A huge fracture in the ice developed, splitting the ice down the center. Luckily, they were on the side closest to Allison, and he quickly skated toward them, giving Cameron and Aiden to her. He turned back around to get Rina and cursed again.

The ice started cracking and dividing into small ice floes, the water sloshing up the sides as if something were forcing it.

Fuck.

This had to be Jack.

He looked over the area and tried to remain calm. They were stranded on an ice floe in the center of the ring, water all around them.

"Rina, don't move!" he called.

"Justin, hurry!" she called back.

He looked around for anything to get to her and cursed. There was nothing.

"Justin, oh, God, Lacy." Allison clutched his sleeve, but he could tell she was trying not to freak out in front of the kids.

"I'm going to call 911. We have service by the cars," Abby said as she gripped both boys' shoulders and took them with her. "I'm taking the boys with me."

Justin nodded but kept his gaze on Rina. He had to act quickly. A sudden gust caused the ice to crack again, and the small patch that the girls were standing on grew smaller. He watched as Rina picked Lacy up and looked at him. She was gonna jump; it was the only way. Allison gripped his sleeve, and he was stuck. There was no way to get to them, not without risking moving the ice by accident and causing Rina to fall in. He watched as Rina jumped over the crevice, throwing Lacy onto the bigger ice floe. Allison ran to the side and reached over a smaller stream of water. Lacy crawled on her hands and knees, tears running down her face, and finally reached her mom. Allison pulled her over the crevice and sat on the snow, holding Lacy in her arms.

Justin had only seen all of this out of the corner of his eye because, as Rina had thrown Lacy to save her life, she'd fallen into the crevice. Without thinking, Justin jumped over another gap in the ice, twisting his ankle in a skate, but shaking off the pain to get to her.

Please, be okay.

He heard her scream as her head went under the ice water and his heart stopped. No, this couldn't be happening. He heard the shouts of others behind him, but he had eyes for only Rina. With the amount of clothes bundled on her, they would be weighing her down quickly. The ice cracked under his skates, and he froze.

Fuck.

He lowered himself to his belly and tried to

shuffle lightly toward her, aware the ice could crack under him at any moment. Her hand stuck out from the icy water again, and she reached out, trying to grab him. Her fingers had barely touched him, but she was too slippery, and she slid back under the water.

"Rina!"

He slid as close as he dared to without causing both of them injury and reached out again.

"Rina! Grab my hand," he yelled.

Her head came to the surface again, but he could tell she was losing energy. No, he couldn't lose her, not when he'd just found her. His heart beat so fast it echoed in his ears, and his body shook as the ice stabbed at him, cold, unrelenting.

Her hand came out one more time, and he gripped it.

Thank God.

Even though his body slid against the ice, he pulled her as hard as he could, knowing he might hurt her, but it was better than the alternative. She came out of the water, gasping, her face blue.

He pulled her into his arms and held her close. Shit, she was like ice. He looked down at her ears and cursed. She didn't even have enough energy to hold up her glamour. He took off her hat and put his on top of her head, hiding her ears.

They had enough to worry about; they didn't need to deal with the fact that the public could find out she was an elf.

"Justin," Rina said, her teeth chattering, her lips blue.

"Shh, baby, I'll get you home."

"No doctors...can't find out..." Her eyes started to close, and he shook her.

"No doctors, Rina, but you need to keep awake. Baby, please."

She opened her eyes, and he lifted her in his arms. His ankle throbbed, and it hurt to skate with her in his arms, but he made his way to a break in the ice and was able to take a large step over it, the ice seeming to come together a bit more.

Jack must have been finished terrorizing them for now.

Bastard.

He was going to kill him.

When he got to the edge, Allison was crying and threw her arms around Justin's shoulders.

"Thank you for saving my babies," she whispered. She kissed his forehead then did the same to Rina's before going back to her children.

Abby rushed to his side as he fell to the ground, out of energy. She helped him hold Rina, both trying to use all of their body heat to keep her warm. He heard sirens as the paramedics showed up.

"Abby, we can't let them know she's an elf," he whispered.

Abby nodded. "We'll have them look over the children and at least take a quick look at Rina. But don't worry, the paramedics know us well enough that they know we'll take good care of her and get her warm."

Abby sweet-talked their way out of a trip to the hospital, and they bundled up Rina and got her in Justin's car. Tyler pulled up right when they were figuring out how they were going to keep her warm.

"Abigail, can you drive Justin's car?" Tyler said without actually looking at Abby.

She nodded but didn't say anything to him.

"Okay, Justin, you hop in the back with Rina and try to get her warm. Abigail can drive, and I'll follow. Then I'll get Abigail home."

It sounded as good as an idea as any, and they all got in their cars and drove to Justin's.

"I'm going to start a lukewarm bath. Will you get her out of her clothes?" Abby said as they got into Justin's house.

Justin nodded and walked up the stairs to their bedroom.

"I'm going get some hot cocoa ready for her and then make you guys something to eat," Tyler called from the kitchen.

Justin didn't say anything as he stripped Rina down. When she stood naked before him, he cursed. Her body wasn't as blue as it was before, and she didn't look in danger as she had before, but he quickly divested himself of his clothing and cursed.

"Abby, I'm getting in the tub with her, so unless you want to see something that would bring us way too close, I suggest you go to the kitchen with Ty."

"I'm really okay not seeing that but be careful."

He heard her move away from the bathroom and walk down the stairs. Carefully, he gathered Rina in his arms and walked into the bathroom.

"Thank you for saving me," Rina whispered.

"I love you."

"I love you too."

He sat her in the front of the bathtub so he could crawl in behind her. The water felt prickly against his skin, and he cursed, thinking of a how it must feel against Rina, who was so much colder.

He pulled her back against him, and she sighed. "I never want to see you in that situation again," he said as he kissed the top of her head.

She gave a dry laugh and sank into his hold. "I never want to *be* in that situation again."

"That sounds good to me."

"Are the kids okay?"

"Yes, Allison said they didn't have a scratch on them. You saved Lacy's life."

"I was so scared, Justin. Why would Jack do this?"

"I don't know, baby, but I'm going to find out."

"I hope so."

They sat in the tub for twenty or so minutes until Tyler called from the other side of the door, telling them that he was going to take Abigail home and that their dinner was warming in the oven on low so they could take their time. When Justin heard the front door shut, he gathered up Rina in his arms and dried them off then dressed them each in some of his old sweats.

"I'm tired."

"I know, baby, but let's get some fuel in you."

They ate a tuna casserole that Tyler had made and left the dishes in the sink, not caring about the mess. When he got them back to the bedroom, Rina turned into his arms and gave him a heated kiss.

"Make love to me, Justin."

His cock pressed against her stomach, and he groaned. "I thought you were tired."

"I'll sleep later. I need you now."

He nodded, and then he took her mouth with his. He needed her more than his next breath, needed to know she was his, alive, whole, and warm. They stripped off their clothes, and he lowered her to the bed, their tongues tangling, their bodies touching in every intimate way.

He reached between them and found her wet, needy for him. He traced her clit with his thumb, and she shuddered. He entered two fingers into her core, and she clamped down on him. Still kissing her, he thrust his fingers in and out, rubbing her clit at the same time. He pulled his lips away and watched her as she came around his hand, her body flushing, her lips puffy and pouting.

Justin needed to be inside her, deeper than before. He licked her sweet taste off his fingers and groaned. Perfect. He got off her and stood at the edge of the bed, and she squirmed.

"Justin, where are you going?"

"Nowhere, baby, but I want to take you deeper."

"Okay," she said as she bit her lip.

He grinned and pulled her to the edge of the bed where he flipped her onto her stomach.

"I like this dominant side of you," she teased and wiggled her butt.

He gave her a slight slap, and she hissed out a moan. "Good to know." He kneaded the globes of her ass, spreading her cheeks. He could see her pussy, wet and pink, ready for his cock.

Thank God he didn't need to use a condom anymore. Using her juices, he covered the tiny little hole that he knew had never been breached for.

"What are you doing?" she said as she tensed.

"I told you; I want to feel every part of you. Don't worry. I'm not gonna take you here, not tonight. But we can play."

"Okay, I trust you."

Slowly, he inserted a finger all the way to

the knuckle, and she tensed. "Breathe out, baby, feel me." She nodded and relaxed, and he slowly worked until he had two fingers inside. When she was panting with need, he finally thrust his cock inside her pussy, slamming to the hilt.

They both moaned, and she called out his name. Alternating between fucking her ass with his fingers and fucking her pussy with his cock, he set a pace that would drive them both to insanity. Their breaths quickened until he could feel her begin to tighten.

"Come for me, Rina."

She came then, her body bowing, milking his cock. He followed right behind her then moved his hands slowly until he could grip her hips. He pushed forward so they were pressed as close as they could be together as his dick finally stopped twitching.

Jesus, he'd been so deep he couldn't even breathe.

When he couldn't stand any more, he pulled out of her slowly. She was still melting at the edge of the bed, her body lax. He smiled. Oh, yes, he loved this woman.

With the last of his energy, he pulled her into his arms then got into the bed with her, wrapping himself around her.

"We need to do that again," she whispered, her naked breasts pressed against his chest.

"Definitely." He kissed her forehead as he felt her fall asleep in his arms. But, he couldn't fall asleep so quickly. Jack had almost killed her and his friends today, again. There was no way Justin could just sit back and let that happen. He would do what he could to protect the woman he loved and the family he wanted them to be, no matter what.

Chapter 10

Rina sat in the middle of the bed looking at her lists and frowned. She rubbed her temples and cracked her neck. Christmas was in three days, and Justin was doing amazing. Ever since she'd almost died, Justin had been tackling the training with a renewed vigor. He could pretty much do the day-to-day things on his own, slowly releasing his energy throughout the day instinctually. For the other things, like their own relationship, they were connected in a way far greater than she'd ever imagined. She just wished she could be sure it would last. With Jack acting the way that he was, she had no idea what her future held. Santa might believe that she was lying about what Jack had done. As punishment, he could remove from her job—and, in doing so, take her away from Justin. She held her stomach and groaned. Too much was up in the air, and it was freaking her out.

It had only been two days since the ice-skating incident, as she called it, and she was finally feeling back to her old self. Her body had regained its warmth when Justin had made love to her with all of his heart. She blushed at the memory of him touching her where she'd been untouched before.

Apparently, she was a naughty elf. What a cliché.

Justin was out Christmas shopping, and he wouldn't let her come with him. She tried not to think of what he might be buying her, if anything. They had only known each other less than a month, and she was already living with him. Things were going a little too fast for her if she thought about it, so she didn't. If she went too deep into the details, she might never come out or, worse, she might rethink herself out of the relationship.

She closed up her notes and went down for a cup of hot cocoa. She and Justin had made a batch of sugar cookies the night before, so she took one, just because it was there, not because she was addicted or anything. She smiled at the thought of Justin's face when he'd taken a bite from one of the cookies straight from the oven. He had a look of such pleasure on his face she'd almost wanted to leave him alone with it. She knew that executives grew a sweet tooth as they came into their powers, but Justin seemed to be taking it in stride. Thank God the magic running through his body burned the calories or he'd be pleasantly plump at this point.

With Christmas almost upon them, her job was coming to a close, unless Santa approved of what Justin had been doing. Then she'd be able to stay. Warmth filled her at the thought of staying with Justin. They hadn't talked about their future past making sure she could stay, but she hoped that life could resume on its current course. The way she and Justin worked together to provide happiness for their town made her think that this could work.

Their town. She didn't know when she'd started to think of Holiday has her town, but she liked the idea of it. Already she felt more at home in the small Montana town than she ever had at the North Pole. She felt needed, wanted. Peppermint sticks, she didn't want to leave.

Jack was out of control, yet no one at the North Pole would take her calls. She couldn't call Santa directly, but she'd at least tried to call the elves surrounding him. But, she'd been shunned. She looked at her hands and tried not to cry. Yes, she might have always felt out of place, but she wouldn't have thought they'd turned their backs on her so completely. She shouldn't have run away and broken the rules the way she had, but she hadn't expected they'd ignore her. People were getting hurt, and Jack was a danger. Yet, because of her mistake and the others' ignorance, she couldn't do anything about it.

Maybe after Christmas she could. It was her only hope, and the town's only hope to escape Jack.

She looked at the clock and sighed. Justin should be coming home soon.

Home.

She liked the thought of this place being her and Justin's home. Since the first time she'd seen it, she'd known that it needed a woman's touch, and now, if things worked out, she would be the one filling his place with warmth.

She loved him.

Slightly bored, Rina stared out the window as the snow started to come down a little bit harder. She hoped Justin made it home soon before the roads got really bad. She stared at the glass and frowned.

Why did it look like it was frosting on the

inside rather than on the outside where the snow was?

She stood up and walked toward the window, unease sliding through her. Something was wrong. She held out her hand, touched the glass, and gasped. The ice was on the inside, not the outside. Maybe there was just a draft.

As soon as that thought crossed her mind, the chill increased, sending goose bumps down her arm. She pulled down her long sleeves and shivered.

"You really shouldn't have tried to contact the other elves," Jack said as he walked down the stairs toward her.

Rina lifted her hands and tried to get a good look at the door from the corner of her eye. Jack stood between her and the only exit, and she inwardly cursed. She lifted her chin but didn't say anything. There was no use in antagonizing him when he had the upper hand.

"Do you have any idea how hard it is to make sure that the elves in my control are the ones to answer your calls? It takes too much of my time having to deal with schedule shifts and other mundane tasks. Luckily, some of my more energetic elves, shall we say, took matters into their own hands."

Jack grinned, and another shiver went down

Rina's spine that had nothing to do with the cold and everything to do with the sadistic glee in his eyes.

"Now that nobody knows that you have issues down here, no one will even care when you're gone."

"You're wrong; people will care," she said before she bit her tongue. She hadn't meant to antagonize him, but she couldn't help herself.

"You are nothing. You're just a little elf with a big mouth. You should have stayed down in the basement where you belonged."

"Why did you put me there in the first place?" If she was going to die, she might as well know exactly why.

Jack flicked his fingers, and the temperature in the room dropped ten degrees. She gripped her arms and held herself, trying to keep the warmth. She knew it wouldn't be of much use soon.

"Why were you in the basement? Because I could place you there. You shouldn't have laughed at me. He shouldn't have said no when I asked you to be mine. Now that I can't have you, no one else gets to have you either. You're a whore for spreading your legs for that peasant. But, no worries. I'll take care of the both of you, and then no one will even remember your name or what you tried to spew about me."

Jack took a step closer, and she shivered again. She could see her breath and see the ice sliding up the walls and doors. Soon it would look like an ice cavern, not the home that Justin had spent so long to build.

"You're doing all of this because I wouldn't go on a date with you?" Fury filled her, warming her somewhat. "You could have killed all of those children because you felt like I hurt your feelings? What kind of monster are you?"

Jack's arm shot out so fast she didn't comprehend what was happening until she flew back into the wall, her cheek stinging from the icy slap.

"Shut up, you little whore. I can do whatever the hell I want. I'm Santa's second-in-command, remember? I can do no wrong. So, don't even think to mess with me. I'm going to enjoy watching you freeze, and then I'm going to kill your little executive the same way. Though not until he sees your frozen corpse."

Rina held her cheek, even as tears spilled onto her face. No, not Justin. There had to be something she could do. She tried to stand up again, but Jack spread ice around her, cementing her to the floor. Her skin prickled where the ice stung and bit in. Her body shivered as the last of its heat did its best to hold on.

She didn't want to die like this.

Powerless.

Useless.

She was an elf, not a human. Why couldn't she use her magic? Oh, yeah, because she was only a funnel of an executive's magic, not magical in her own right.

"Why did you come to Holiday?" she asked, her breath rasping at the stark coldness.

Jack crouched down to her eye level and traced an icy finger along her bruising cheekbone. She flinched, and he slapped her again. Pain shocked her, and her body shook.

"I'm here because your little man is in my way."

"What?" She coughed.

"You don't think this is all about you, do you? No, I've been working for years trying to get to the top. Santa is an old man, and it's time for him to step down. I'm going to lead, and I'm going to have the power, but in order to do that, I need to get rid of the one man who could ruin it all for me."

"What?" she said, her teeth chattering.

"Justin holds too much power. Why do you think I was going to let him slide through the cracks?"

"It was you? You were the one who changed his file and didn't let him know about his role?"

"Of course, and everything was going fine until you came along and fucked it up."

He traced his finger over her lips, and she shuddered in revulsion.

Her body shook violently, the ice surrounding her growing jagged, painful as it pricked her skin. She looked around and let out a moan. Ice covered every inch of the house, making it look like an iced castle, dangerous in its beauty.

"You can't take over the North Pole; the others won't let you."

"Don't worry about my plans. I'll make do. I always do. You, on the other hand, should be worrying about yourself."

Her eyelids grew heavy, and her body was growing too cold, not sustaining enough energy to keep her awake.

No, she had to stay awake. For Justin.

"I'm sorry you had to die this way, but you got in my way," Jack whispered. At least she thought he did. Everything seemed so far away.

She closed her eyes, her body cold, iced. A shout and a crash shook her awake. She willed herself to pry open her eyes, expending the last of her energy.

"You bastard!" Justin called as he slammed his fist into Jack's face.

Yes, he was here. He'd take care of Jack and save her people, their town.

Jack moved forward, spitting out blood from Justin's punch. "You're too late. You're little whore is dead, and you're nothing compared to me. I'm going to enjoy watching you freeze from the outside in. The blood in your veins will turn to slush while your eyes bulge. Yes, I can't wait."

No, Justin was stronger; Jack had said so. Justin just needed to use his magic and try. Rina lifted her head and opened her mouth to speak, but her body was too heavy, too cold.

She couldn't be weak. Justin needed her. Maybe if she acted like his funnel again, she could help him. Though they weren't touching, she knew their connection might be strong enough for it to work. She focused inward, looking for that thread of magic that connected her to the love of her life.

There. She felt a pulsating link to Justin, weak, cold, but there.

"Justin," she croaked. "You're stronger than he is. Use that."

Justin pulled a punch from Jack's face and, turned to her, relief and surprise on his face. Oh,

God, he'd thought she was dead. She could be soon though. Jack scowled and tried to reach for Justin's neck, but Justin ducked, hitting Jack square in the stomach. Jack groaned and let out a breath of surprise before Justin ran the other man into the wall.

Justin nodded and released his magic. Though he could do it daily, she knew he was using his reserves to help her. It flooded her system, warming her to the core. Energized, she tunneled out his magic and focused on Jack. Jack snarled and threw his magic back at the two of them.

Ice met warmth.

Justin staggered back and took the few steps to be by her side. She knew that they could make their magic work when they weren't touching, even though it wouldn't be as strong, but connected, they could beat Jack. They had to. Justin gripped her hand, her body still frozen and stuck to the floor.

When their fingers touched, magic poured from both of them, and Jack screamed. Though other people liked the warmth and magic she and Justin gave, Jack wouldn't. His body was made of ice, cold and deadly. Their magic warmed him and brought with it Jack's own magic that caused a rippling and tearing throughout his body. She turned and looked into Justin's deep blue eyes and focused all her energy, breaking Jack's icy connection.

Sweat dripped from Justin's brow, and she shivered again because she was still so cold. The ice around them melted to a pool of water, drenching everything in its wake. They tangled their fingers together, their magic flowing through them, connected, and right. Jack fell to his knees, the ice around him melting into a pool. Water dripped from the walls, spreading onto the floor. The house shook under the force of all the moving energy, but she didn't let go of Justin's hand. She couldn't.

Justin squeezed her hand harder and pushed more magic through her, his body straining, hers shaking. Jack fell to his back, his body convulsing. He shot off his magic and it reversed back toward him. Ice covered his body in a slow crawl until he was completely immobile.

Rina let out a deep breath and looked down at herself. When Jack had frozen his magic, the ice surrounding her had melted away. Justin pulled her into his arms, and she kissed him, hard.

"Oh, God, Rina, I thought I'd lost you." He kissed her again then ran his hands up and down her body looking for broken bones. When he traced his fingers over her cheek, he winced. "He hurt you."

"I'm fine, thanks to you."

"No, thanks to you." He kissed her again, and she sank into him.

"Damn, we were too late," a familiar voice said from the doorway, and she turned toward it. Justin placed himself in front of her, blocking her from the intruder.

"Isaac?" she asked the elf who stood there. No, the elves had shunned her and couldn't be here.

"Rina?" Isaac asked. "Damn, I'm so sorry we're so late."

"What are you doing here?" she asked.

"Who are you?" Justin asked, annoyance in his tone.

The male elf took off his hat, his pointy ears prevalent. "My apologies. I'm Isaac, and I worked with Rina."

Justin stood on shaky legs and glared. "Well, your piece-of-shit boss is right over there underneath his own ice. I would go take care of him if I were you. Where the hell were you when Rina needed you before?"

"Justin, it's okay." She stood behind him and leaned on his back.

He turned quickly and pulled her into his arms. "No, it's not okay."

Isaac gestured to the other elves behind him, and they took Jack into custody and carried his frozen body out of the house. Even though Jack could manipulate ice, she didn't think he'd be okay being surrounded by it like he was. She didn't know what they were going to do with him, but she was glad it wasn't her problem anymore.

"Justin, they were just doing their job. They didn't know about Jack."

"I don't fucking care. You could have died because they let this man run around like he was a god."

Isaac cleared his throat. "I'm truly sorry. We've been keeping an eye on him in the North Pole for a while now, but we had no idea he was this bad. Honest. It wasn't until the elves under his control started to attack our own elves that we knew there was a bigger problem." The elf wiped his brow and shifted from foot to foot. "We've been so busy with the Christmas preparations that we almost let a whole town and one of our own be destroyed by a monster. I'm truly sorry."

Tears filled Rina's eyes, and she nodded, too choked up to speak. Justin hugged her tighter, and she nuzzled into his chest.

"Take care of her, Justin," Isaac said as he walked out of the house. "Your magic will be able to repair the damage to your belongings. I just hope that you can find it in yourselves to forgive us. Christmas is in two days, so you know we'll be busy, but when it's over, I know Santa will be around to talk to you."

She stiffened at the harsh reminder of her stupidity for taking things into her own hands and coming to Holiday.

"Thank you," Justin gritted between clenched teeth. "Take your iced man and leave, please."

The other elf nodded and closed the door behind him. Justin held her close, his warmth seeping into her, keeping her steady.

"I'll do whatever it takes to keep you here with me," he whispered.

She nodded, unable to speak. If only his words would be enough.

Chapter 11

Rina stood on Justin's porch, welcoming the cold, knowing it wasn't from Jack. Once the elves had left yesterday, Justin had held her hand and quickly warmed up his house, driving away all evidence of Jack's presence. He hadn't even had to ask how to do it. Jack had been right. Justin was stronger than any other executive she'd ever heard of. Pride filled her at the thought of Justin being so talented, but at the same time, she still felt a little weak. Yes, the fact that she could handle all his magic proved that she was stronger also, and she had given herself some credit for it, but she still hadn't been able to fight Jack on her own.

In retrospect, she thought Justin might not have been able to fight Jack on his own either. They were a team. If only Santa would realize that and let her stay. With Christmas just around the corner, she knew her time might be limited. Even though she should have been inside with Justin, savoring what could be her last moments, she wanted to stay outside in the cold for just a little longer.

Jack was gone. Not dead, but not fully awake anymore either. The other elves said he'd put himself into a stasis when the magic had backfired on him. Rina wasn't sorry about what had happened to Jack, though she wished there had been another way to go about it. Now, Jack's frozen body was tucked away in a magically protected prison. If he ever did wake up on his own, he wouldn't be able to go anywhere. That, at least, was a small comfort.

Justin was inside on the phone with his brother Jackson while she sat on the porch. He'd already talked to the rest of his brothers, and Jackson was the last one. Justin had refused his brothers' offers of help to finish up the cleaning that the magic hadn't been able to get. There was really nothing they could do. With the holidays coming right around the corner, Justin wanted them to stay away, knowing he would see them soon. Once he'd convinced his brothers that coming to his home would accomplish nothing at the moment, he had carried her upstairs in his arms and made love to her until the sun had come up.

Her body still tingled with the memories of his fingers tracing every inch of her, making sure she was okay. She'd do anything to make that permanent. She wanted to wake up in Justin's arms every morning and grow old with him. Just the thought of that should've sent fear through her. They'd known each other only a month, and yet she couldn't help but think of a future with him.

"Why are you sitting out in the cold, little elf?" a deep voiced asked from the porch, startling her out of her thoughts.

No, it couldn't be.

"Santa?"

"You can call me Kris you know. After all, you saved us from the man I couldn't," Kris Kringle said as he came into view. He wore old jeans and a flannel shirt that looked warm and comfortable. He was about as tall as the Cooper brothers, and he had their build.

No matter what people thought Santa looked like, she could bet most people didn't think of him as he was—a sexy man who looked to be in his fifties. Nope, no way.

"You aren't wearing your glamour," she said. *Oops, that was rude.* But, it was the first thing that popped into her mind.

Kris sat next her on the bench and sighed. "No, I didn't think I could blend in with that jolly image. I think I'm the only person whose glamour makes him look worse than the real thing."

"Kids love it, though."

He grinned, and Rina held her breath. Yep, even without the glamour, he still had that same smile that made people fall in love with him and children want to believe in happiness. This was why he was Santa, not because of the presents, but because he was happiness personified when he wanted to be.

"True. Mrs. Kringle chose my glamour when we first started this all those years ago, and I couldn't say no to her. I *still* can't say no to her. I guess that's what happens when you fall in love." He winked at her, and she blushed.

"Christmas is in two days. What are you doing here? Don't you have work to do?" she asked, knowing that he was here for a reason and not just to talk about his wife.

"Of course, Rina, dear, but I trust my elves to do their jobs. Well, I used to. Now, I'm not so sure."

She bit her lip and lowered her gaze as shame filled her.

He reached over and lifted her chin with his finger. "I'm talking about those elves who threw their lot in with Jack, not you. You did what you had to in order to protect Justin. I understand that."

"But, I thought I was going to be punished."

He shook his head and leaned back onto the bench. "No, I think what Jack did is more than enough punishment." He let out a sigh. "I was only going to make you clean out a closet of gift wrapping or something. Jack almost killed you. I'm so sorry, Rina."

"I forgive you," she said as she wrapped her arms around herself. "Though, it wasn't really your fault."

"Yes, it was. And to try and make up for it, I'm going to make this job of yours permanent."

Excitement filled her. "Really?"

Kris winked. "Really. You deserve it."

"I didn't know we had company," Justin said from the doorway.

She sat up and looked at him. He was

leaning against the doorframe and had his arms crossed in front of him. He also had a glare on his face that she didn't quite understand.

"Justin, this is Kris."

Kris Kringle smiled at them both and shook his head. "You can also call me Santa. So, get that glare off your face. I don't have any designs on your girl."

Justin visibly relaxed as a blush crept up his neck.

She bit back a laugh. "You were jealous of Santa Claus?"

Justin snorted then moved to sit on her other side. "All I saw was a man I didn't know on my porch talking to you and touching you. I'm sorry."

She smiled then kissed him softly. "You're forgiven."

Justin shifted to hold out his hand to Santa. The two men shook then leaned back.

"So, you're my boss," Justin said as he toyed with a strand of her hair. Tendrils of pleasure shot up her spine, but she still glared at him. Santa was sitting right next to her, and Justin was trying to turn her on.

Darn man.

"Yep, and you're the young man I saved all those years ago."

Justin nodded, a look of sadness passing over his face. "Thank you for that."

"You deserved to live, Justin."

"How could you tell though? I was just some punk kid."

Rina gripped Justin's hand but didn't say anything. She knew this was something Justin needed to get out there, and Santa was the only one who could help him.

"I saw in here." Santa put a hand over his heart. "You're a good person, Justin. You always were. I'm just glad I was there to help."

"Thank you."

"Thank you for taking care of Jack and Rina. There's nothing I can say except to ask for your forgiveness for not taking down Jack all those years ago. But, I thank you for helping when I couldn't. I'd thought he changed. I was wrong."

"It's not your fault Jack is who he is," Rina said. "You showed him what it meant to be a good person, but he followed his own path."

Santa nodded but said nothing.

After a pause, Santa turned to Justin. "So,

Justin, I'm sure you're curious about your job throughout the year."

Justin shrugged. "Pretty much. I mean, the holidays are over after this right?"

Santa smiled and winked. "You'd think, but not so much. Your job is to make sure people keep happiness alive. It's not as strong as it is during the holidays, but the need is still there. The holidays aren't the only time when people can show their good will toward one another and feel the goodness of others. You can still help those less fortunate. You just don't have to help with the magic of Christmas Eve's gifts."

Justin nodded and smiled. "So, in other words, help when I can and keep Rina by my side?"

Santa smiled and nodded while Rina buried into Justin's side. Yeah, she liked that part the most.

After a few more minutes, Rina shivered then cursed. "Why are we sitting outside?"

Justin laughed. "Because you're cute when you're flustered. Let's go in and get some hot cocoa."

"Yum."

"I'm going to leave you to that," Santa said as he got up from the bench. "I have a lot of traveling coming up soon." He winked then left without another word. She watched as Santa took two steps of the porch, then took out a miniature snow globe and vanished in a blur of snow and lights.

Justin gathered her up in his arms and carried her into the house. She rested her head on his shoulder and sighed.

"Have I told you how much I love when you act all manly and carry me places in the house?"

He kissed her forehead then set her on the counter. "I like it, too."

"So, it looks like I'm going to be your assistant for a while."

Justin nodded but didn't say anything. Isn't that what he'd wanted? She bit her lip but didn't voice her concern.

What if Justin didn't want her to stay now?

****

Justin stood in the foyer at Jackson's house and ate the rest of his sugar cookie. It was Christmas Day, and the Coopers, Jordan, Rina, and Abby were having a huge dinner to celebrate.

Even though Justin wanted to be in there with them, he didn't feel comfortable. Ever since Santa had left him and Rina on the porch, things had been awkward. He loved her more than he'd ever thought possible, but he didn't know if being here was what she wanted. She had the whole world at her fingertips, and now she could be stuck with him.

Was it fair to Rina to make her stay?

He licked the frosting off his finger and closed his eyes. He didn't think he was strong enough to let her go either. He loved her. Was that enough?

"What are you doing out here?" Rina asked as she walked to his side. She didn't reach for his hand, and he knew it was his fault. He was acting like an ass, and now she didn't know where they stood. He'd drawn into himself and hadn't spoken to her as he had before Jack's attack. She hated not knowing where she stood.

"Just thinking," he finally answered.

"Oh," she said and turned to leave. He gripped her hand and pulled her into his arms.

"I'm sorry, baby." He framed her face with his hands and kissed her softly.

"What's going on, Justin? Don't you want me anymore?"

He closed his eyes as shame filled him. "Of course I do. I want you with every ounce of my being."

"Then why are you pushing me away?" She pulled back, but he kept his hands on her, unable to relinquish the feel of her.

"Don't you want to see the world? I mean you don't have to be here. I don't want to keep you here if it's not what you want."

Rina looked at him and blinked. Then she pulled away and let out a frustrated scream. "You're kidding, right? You're acting like an ass because you're thinking *for* me?"

"Uh..."

"You think that just because I can leave you, I will? You're an idiot!"

"Rina—"

"No, shut up. You listen to me, Justin Cooper. I love you. You and I are a freaking team. If you didn't learn that from what went down with Jack, you're an idiot. I cannot believe you think I'd leave you at the first chance I got. What the heck do you think I love you means?"

Justin let out a breath and pulled her into his arms. She fought for a second before sinking into his hold. "I'm sorry, baby. I just don't want you to be stuck with me."

She glared then bit the underside of his chin. "I could never be stuck with you. I actually like being with you. You dork."

"I promise never to think for you again."

She threw her head back and laughed. "Yeah, I don't believe you, baby. You're a man, but it's okay. I love you."

"I love you, too."

He nipped at her lip then kissed her, hard. She wrapped her arms around his neck, and he pressed her against the wall. Their breaths came in heavy pants as he ground his hips against hers. She moaned into his mouth, and he cupped her breast, rolling her nipple in his fingers.

"For the love of God, do not have sex in my house," Jackson yelled.

Justin and Rina pulled apart, their breathing ragged, their clothes mussed. Justin cleared his throat, and Rina blushed. "Sorry, man."

"Get presentable and get in here. We have presents to open, and I don't have the inclination for another couple getting it on at my house." He winked then left them alone.

He never could understand his brother, but damn, he loved the man.

"I can't believe we almost had sex in your brother's house with the rest of your family right next to us."

Justin smiled, gave her a quick kiss on her swollen lips, and pulled her to the living room. The rest of the family gave them knowing looks, but he ignored them, trying to save Rina at least some embarrassment.

He sat back against a chair, and Rina sat between his legs. Bray stood off to the side, helping Jackson remove the presents from under the tree and handing them to the named person. Matt sat on the couch with Jordan draped on top of him as he played with her hair and opened gifts. While Rina sat on the floor next to him, Abby bounced up and down as she opened each gift. She smiled at each of them and said her thanks for the gifts. She really was like a sister to them.

Well, maybe not to everyone. Tyler sat in an armchair across from them, a glare on his face. He unwrapped his gifts, but Justin noticed that he didn't really look at anything he opened. Justin didn't know what was going on, but Tyler needed to get over whatever it was with Abby and grow up. They were a family.

Rina snuggled into his hold, and he kissed her temple. "Are you having a good Christmas?"

She smiled up at him. "You're not so bad after all, Justin Cooper."

He leaned down and kissed her softly. "As long as I have you, I don't need to be."

The End

ABOUT THE AUTHOR

Carrie Ann Ryan is a bestselling paranormal and contemporary romance author. After spending too much time behind a lab bench, she decided to dive into the romance world and find her werewolf mate - even if it's just in her books. Happy endings are always near - even if you have to get over the challenges of falling in love first.

Carrie Ann's Redwood Pack series is a bestselling series that has made the shifter world even more real to her and has allowed the Dante's Circle and Holiday, Montana series to be born. She's also an avid reader and lover of romance and fiction novels. She loves meeting new authors and new worlds. Any recommendations you have are appreciated. Carrie Ann lives in New England with her husband and two kittens.

Printed in Great Britain
by Amazon